CADENCE

A DECEPTION NOVEL, BOOK 2

BY BEST SELLING AUTHORS
D.H. SIDEBOTTOM & KER DUKEY

Other Books by the authors

FaCade (Deception series Book 1)

Other Books by the DH Sidebottom

Shocking Heaven (Room 103)
Thrilling Heaven (Room 103)
Denying Heaven (Room 103)
Finally Heaven (Room 103)

Incineration (NSC Industries Book 1)
Tolerance (NSC Industries Book 2)
Resolution (NSC Industries Book 3)
Atonement (NSC Industries Book 4)

The Decimation of Mae (The Blue Butterfly Book 1)
The Salvation of Daniel (The Blue Butterfly Book 2)

Fragile Truths (The Shadows of Sin Book 1)

Other titles by Ker Dukey

The Broken
The Broken Parts Of Us
The Broken Tethers That Bind Us

My Soul Keeper

The Beats In Rift

Empathy

DEDICATION

TO OUR DEPRAVED READERS WHO WANT TO BE
MRS TROY.
YOU'RE TWISTED, KINKY AND JUST LIKE US.

WE **FUCKING** LOVE YOU.
THIS ONE'S FOR YOU.

PROLOGUE

Cade

FAYE. GOD, SHE WAS THERE again in my dreams, so vivid I could smell her scent.

"Argh!"

I smothered my face in her pillow, the one I TRAVELED with. I didn't give a fuck if that made me a pussy. Yeah, I was a film star but I was also human and I was dying inside without her.

My body wept and my heart beat out of my chest. I wanted the crippling throb to ease so I could focus on anything but the hole in the pit of my stomach that swallowed another piece of me every day I woke up without her. I wanted to be set free from the constant ache I'd felt since the day they told me her plane went down.

I loved her then, and my love for her now was killing me slowly.

Men are funny creatures. We love fiercely when we find the right woman. Family, friends . . . none of it matters when you have the one. We fly the nest and our love and life, our *everything,* revolves around the love we harbor for our woman. Don't get me wrong, I loved my family and friends but if it came down to a choice she would have won every time.

I didn't need anyone but her. Men don't need much to function. It's true what they say; you only need the love of a good woman. I had

1

that and lost it.

I couldn't believe she was gone. If she was dead I would have felt it, I would have ceased to exist. I was barely existing now; an apparition of my former self. I was breathing but not really present in the world. My heart was dying. There was still a beat but no sound.

Thoughts tore at my mind. Was she scared? The sound of the crash, the twisting and crunching of metal, the whooshing of air as it was sucked from the cabin, the heat from the fire that lit up the engine on impact. My beautiful girl; scared, screaming and crying. Did she think about me as fear took hold of her and held her in its grip?

They found no bodies. They said the fire was too bad and refused to allow us the pictures. I knew my woman was still out there. My soul was tethered to hers and it still sensed her essence. I would find her. I would never rest until I found her.

My phone buzzed, startling me. I reached across the bed and grabbed my cell. My best friend, Jenson, had finally text.

I have someone willing to take us to the location of the crash site. Be ready in one hour

At last, progress. I would start there.

AN HOUR LATER I WAITED outside my hotel room for Jenson. I pulled my baseball cap further down over my sunglasses and tightened the hoody so my lips and nose were barely on show. I looked like a weirdo but that meant people stayed away. I couldn't risk being recognized by a fan.

I ignored the heat as it soaked into the black fibers and made sweat pool in every pore. I sighed in relief when Jenson pulled up in a van, until he gestured for me to get in the back. My brow scrunched but I was too anxious to argue. I opened the door and got in.

A scrawny guy sat in the back looking like someone was about to jump out and shank him. He was nervous, his eyes moving rapidly, his teeth worrying his bottom lip.

I shut the door and ignored the guy itching at his arm like something was crawling under his skin. I was in the film industry and Jenson was a famous rock star. I knew a tweaker when I was shut in a van with one.

"Please tell me you're not our tour guide?"

He looked up at me, then away, shaking his head. "No tour needed, sir." Sir? I didn't think anyone had ever called me *sir* before. I waved my hand in a continue gesture. I was being irritated at breakneck speed. "I work out in the field where this plane crash happened. It's a vineyard. I pick grapes, sir. We were told not to come into work that day but I left something there the day before and I needed it, so I crept in." His eyes kept darting to the door like he was waiting for it to fly open. What the hell was he scared of? His hand went back to tearing into his flesh. "A plane landed in the field, it was amazing. I have never seen a plane up close before."

My heart was on a rampage, raging war with my ribcage. "When you say *landed,* you mean crashed?"

He stared straight at me, his eyes finding focus as he leaned forward. "There was no crash, sir. The plane landed perfectly and a car came. Men went on board and came out with a woman. She was unconscious and then they placed her in the car."

My woman, my fiancée, the love of my life was alive . . . but taken, which meant she could be found and whoever had stolen what was mine would die painfully, choking on his own blood.

I couldn't breathe. The anger, fear and relief all bombarded me at once. There was no air. My phone vibrated against my leg, grounding me. I slipped it free but the number was unknown.

"Who's this?"

I heard a gasp then a drop of the phone. Then . . . her!

"I'm sorry. I'm going to get ready now."

I scrambled to loosen the hood, pulling off my hat and glasses, trying to suck in oxygen. My Faye.

"Faye . . . Faye . . ."

The line was dead.

The tweaker's audible gasp brought me back. God, of course he would recognize me, fucking figures. Why was he scrambling for the door? Usually they scrambled towards me.

3

Turning to me, his head shook from side to side as his wide eyes filled with fear and confusion. "You were there. Is this a test? Please don't kill me."

Shit, he was tripping out on something; a bad batch of whatever he pumped into those veins. He was so pale you'd have thought the Devil had appeared to him.

"Dude, relax, you're about to stroke out." I moved towards him but he flinched and started crying. I banged on the adjoining wall to get Jenson's attention.

I heard his door open and close before the back of the van opened. The tweaker spilled free, landing in a heap at Jenson's feet. "It is him! He killed Rahul and stole the woman!"

It took five seconds for it to register. A further two for me to collapse to my knees. And one more before his name left my lips in disbelief. My brother . . . my twin brother . . . "Dante!"

CHAPTER 1

HEARTACHE

Star Faye

'PLEASE FUCK ME, MR. TROY.'
'Please fuck me, Mr. Troy.'
'Please fuck me, Mr. Troy.'

My insides were disintegrating, I was dying. He wasn't lying. It was all there like a horror movie playing back at me. The pleasure on my face a betrayal to Cade, to us, to what we were to become. Did I deserve this? I knew loving Cade after loving Dante would cause people to talk, but no one knew what we went through. No one knew how much it hurt when he left and never looked back, and all for what? A misunderstanding. I waited. I shouldered the guilt of what I felt needed to be done for Dante to have a better future and this was what he had done with it.

He was so far gone. Broken beyond repair. He functioned on depravity, humiliation, power and retribution for something that never even happened. What a waste of life, of a son, a brother and a man I would have loved forever.

"Turn it off. You've made your point!"

I glowered and he gestured to Malik with a chin jerk to turn it off, his grip on my arm loosening to release me. My mind was retelling my entire life in snap shots blinking image after image, memories happy and sad rapidly into the forefront of my mind causing a headache to form. I needed to be away from him. I needed to let this all sink in and I needed a plan because there was no way in hell I was marrying him and giving him a child to raise.

I needed Cade. *Cade!* Emotions overflowed in me, buckling my legs. My heart fractured inside my chest. He loved me . . . what did he think happened? The reporter mentioned a plane crash. Oh, God! Dante was so twisted!

"Plane crash?" I hiccupped on the sorrow crawling up my throat. His answering smirk caused goose bumps to scatter over my pale skin. I looked and felt like a ghost. He had sucked the life from me. The pain was so explosive it ricocheted through every fiber, destroying me. I loved this man. I gave him seven years. I knew he was possessive, but cruel? Evil? No, this wasn't the man who left; this man had fed on hate and spite and morphed into a monster.

"Poetic, no? You all thought I had died in the plane I should have been on. My own family just accepted the loss! No surprise they accepted yours too!" Leaning down he palmed my face in his grip, forcing me to stare into the angry black abyss of his gaze.

"He just accepted your death! The fucking weasel was always the weak one! He doesn't care about you. He just wanted what was mine! He hated that I was superior to him."

"Cade loves you, Dante! You're his brother. He never once made a move on me when we were together!"

His features contorted into a sneer and he pushed me away from him. "He always looked at you like a lost puppy! He planned to take you from me. Acting all fucking whipped and coming to your aid WHEN YOU SHOULD HAVE COME TO ME!"

His anger ignited the atmosphere, every hair rising on my body. My instincts controlled my movements making me back away, one arm wrapping around my stomach to protect the life inside. His eyes flared as he stalked towards me. "You don't need to protect my child from ME!"

6

Malik grasped Dante's shoulder.

"Take your fucking hand off me if you want to keep it."

"The press will be here any second. That reporter was just the start," Malik warned.

My insides churned and my head was fuzzy with the overload, too much happening and too much knowledge suddenly available at the same time. I couldn't process everything.

"This isn't real."

I laughed. I couldn't stop it from pouring out of me, my hysterical cackles loud in the mounting silence. Tears stained my cheeks and my stomach muscles tightened and ached.

"Shit, she broke." Malik sighed, making me laugh even more until my giggles became shattered sobs.

"This isn't real. I died, or I'm dreaming. Argh! Wake me up!" I dragged myself to my feet; both men were looking at me with furrowed brows but they weren't real. "Cade! Wake me up! Wake me up!" I crashed my fists down on the chest of the man wearing Cade's beautiful face. "Wake me up!" My screams left my throat burning.

The hit to my cheek shocked me silent. The knuckles from his backhanded slap impacted my cheekbone, leaving a violent throb. He caught me before I could fall.

"Calm down," he warned. "And Star . . ." I turned my head to him. "Don't ever call me by his name again. You need to pull yourself together. You have a press release to prepare for!"

My mouth dropped open. There was no way I could do that; I didn't even know what I was going to say.

"You tell them everything has been a misunderstanding and you took some time off to prepare for a secret wedding. You've been on this island off the grid so you didn't know of any news of a plane crash and have kept in contact with your agent who kept all this from you."

My head was spinning, my body shaking. His grip tightened on my arms. "You will tell them that or we play them the footage. What would everyone think of their little starlet then? Crawling around like a dog. Pissing herself and then begging me to fuck her. What would Cade think of you getting off on being used and watched like a filthy whore?"

My heart squeezed too tightly, despair gnawing at my insides. "I hate you! I don't deserve this, Dante! What happened to you?"

"You happened!"

I remembered a different man. A storm had started brewing when we were together, the grey clouds gathered with his moods, but it was nothing compared to the black skies that eclipsed the Dante before me now. A man who broke his friend's hand. A man who killed.

"I'll tell the police you killed Theo!"

His hand moved to my throat, his breath heating my face as he spoke in a deathly quiet voice. "Did I? Prove it." Oh, God. Was he lying about killing Theo? Was that monster still out there? "I'll let Theo have you if you don't do as you're told."

Bile rose, filling my mouth.

"Dante she's choking." Malik's voice echoed in my thoughts as a fuzzy hue stole my sight. I was released from the deadly grip, vomit spewing onto the floor.

"I warned you."

My eyes shot up to see Dante grab Malik's hand from his shoulder and pin it to the table. No one had time to react when the letter opener rose in Dante's other hand and plunged down into Malik's.

Then the hue stole me completely.

CHAPTER 2

NEED

Cade

I FELT JENSON'S EYES ON me as Frank, Taylor and Sed filed into the hotel room. I knew he saw the side of me that had been hidden for years; the monster that resided in the darkest parts of me, slowly peeling back my skin from the inside and crawling to the surface. I didn't stop it; I needed that side of me for what was to come.

I knew this wasn't going to be easy, but to be honest, I was hoping it wasn't. My body craved bloodshed, yearning for a reason to rip some fucker to shreds and watch their pain morph into agony. That side of me crept closer and I became jittery with the rage simmering inside.

Dante was the academic and I was more the "rough around the edges" type. I coasted through School I dabbled in drugs and alcohol, partied hard on the weekends with Jenson and our friends. This consisted of bare knuckle fighting, beer flowing on tap, and girls eager to please; sometimes in twos or threes. The thing about teenage boys is when they can't have the one they want, they have many of the ones they can.

Jenson's folks were always away, leaving him the keys to their castle. That's no joke; his place really was like a castle. His family came from old money. They'd nearly stroked out when Jenson came home with a blond Mohawk and told them he'd started his now extremely successful band, Beneath Innocence. I used to play with them but took the acting route like my father. It was an easy path to go down and made me incredibly rich, incredibly fast.

My passion though, was fighting. I held titles in Taekwondo and kickboxing. I nearly followed my dream into ultimate fighting; that was until Faye gave me her heart. I couldn't risk watching it stop every time I stepped in the ring.

I wanted to fund other young up and coming fighters. Give someone else opportunities they may never otherwise get. I could be around what I loved, with who I loved, and not worry.

Damn, I missed her. My insides were left numb since I found out she was alive. I didn't want to let myself feel too much until I could touch her again, and wrap her in the safety of my embrace and never let her leave it again.

I greeted the guys, mine and Faye's personal security, as they prepared their weapons, each of them as eager as me to get Faye back where she belonged. Frank was close to her; she was like a daughter to him and he would have given up his life for her.

"Still no word from Theo," Frank said without lifting his eyes from his numerous firearms laid out on the bed before him. His tone confirmed his thoughts.

"You think he's sold her out?"

"Yep." His usual simple answer made my heart snarl. The fucking cunt! I knew he was a little runt, just in this business for money, not love and loyalty to Faye, but fuck. The bastard. He would also be on the list.

"Then he is included." I looked at each of them, their simple nods confirming my command. "I don't care who takes who, but I want Dante. He's mine. Is that clear?"

A round of acknowledgements announced their allegiance, except for Jenson who was still quiet.

I turned to him, my brow quirked in question. "You need to say something, Jen, then say it."

"You know I love you, man. You know I would do anything for you."

"But?" I pressed when he swallowed back what he wanted to say.

"But . . ." He cringed slightly then blanked his face to say what I would allow only him as my best friend to say. "It's Dante, Cade. You know how she felt about him. What if . . ."

"If she still loves him?" He nodded, watching my face for a reaction. I pulled back the anger; the need to punish him for releasing his thoughts was overpowering. "I know Faye better than anyone in this room, or the fucking world for that matter." My temper built and I clenched my fists to rein it in. "She would let me know. She's the most honest person I know. Her guilt was thick when we first got together, even after years of waiting for Dan . . . that cunt. There is no way she would just leave me for him, especially without talking to me first."

He nodded but didn't hide his skepticism. "Okay. It's just . . ."

"I've got him!" Kenny shouted from his place at the back of the room, his fingers still thrashing the keyboard of his laptop. Kenny, the lead guitarist for Jenson's rock group, was a whiz at anything technical, from hacking into the most secret of government files to software programming. He was poached by the CIA straight out of high school but preferred to piss them off rather than help them. He was a complete stoner but also a freaking genius. It had been his underhand dealings with high up people who required bank accounts hacking and altering, secret files discovering or even people finding that had provided Jenson's group with the money to start up their band when Jenson's parents stopped funding his lifestyle.

He'd frantically worked for the last two hours, trying to find out where Dante could be.

A map was displayed on his screen; numerous graphical lines criss-crossed over it as multiple coded lines scrolled up the right hand side of the monitor.

Kenny tapped his finger on a small square icon that had zeroed in on what looked like a large building on a remote island south of Cyprus.

"This is the nearest building to the site where Faye was taken from the plane. They could have boarded another plane elsewhere but

I wouldn't have thought so. Taking into account what the tweaker said, I reckon this is it. It has an alarm system that leaves a trace because it's made by a modest fuck who likes to leave a signature imprint." He grinned over at Jenson.

"Martha?"

"The one and only."

Martha, or Blue as she was better known, was a security designer and most of her work wasn't legit. She liked to dabble in the criminal side of the law from time to time but she was the best at her type of work. She made all of Jenson's and the band's security software and it cost a fortune because her systems were supposed to be impenetrable. Fortunately and unfortunately for Jenson, her panties were very much the opposite. He had it bad for her and she had it bad for everyone.

"Can you get her here?" I asked.

He flinched before nodding. "I'll call her now."

My stomach jumped in excitement, my fingers itching with the need to touch my woman. I stared at the small icon, knowing she was there; right there. Not buried under plane rubble, not a burnt out corpse, not even drowned in the sea. She was alive, and stupidly, staring at the location even if it wasn't actually her made me feel as close to her as I had in recent months.

"Cade."

I turned to Jenson. He was staring at the TV, his eyes wide before they flicked back to me. I followed his gaze back to the screen. My knees buckled as my heart slammed against my chest, the beat soaring into dangerous territory. My eyes burned as they focused on my beautiful fiancé.

I stumbled across the room, grabbing the TV remote and increasing the volume. She sat on a dark leather couch, her stunning eyes sad but her face smiling.

"Miss Avery," someone out of shot, presumably the interviewer, said. "May I call you Faye?"

"Of course," Faye smiled softly; the sight made my heart pang.

"Faye, there has been some speculation as to why you disappeared, not least that your plane crashed and you had . . . died. Could you tell us what happened? I take it you are unaware of the media storm around this?"

"Firstly," Faye said with a sigh, "I would like to apologize sincerely to everyone who thought I had died." Her eyes held the camera and I knew she was talking to me, hope in her eyes, sadness and despair in her expression. My throat hurt as I battled with the need to cry out, the scream in my gut trying to force itself free.

"My agent gave me no idea of the hysteria back home. I am not excusing myself, but I am holding him responsible for this. He was alerted to my vacation and . . ."

I blinked. Vacation? She was on her way to an audition. What the fuck?

"So you simply took a vacation?" the woman asked.

Faye stalled for a moment, her eyes flicking upwards to the corner of the screen as though she was looking at someone. "Yes." I read the lie in her face and the stutter in her answer.

"Just a vacation?"

I frowned, growing irritated with the interviewer's need for something juicy, and as much as I wanted to protect my girl from the questions, I also needed the answers. My heart was still beating too fast, my dick stirring as it always did at the sight of Faye. Her perfect legs were crossed at the knee with a small expanse of her creamy thighs on show. Her thick hair was piled on her head and it broke my heart to see her so . . . okay. I'd expected her to be at least a bit out of sorts. She had been kidnapped after all. But then I reminded myself that Faye had won The Best International Actress award three times in a row. She knew how to put on a performance and this is what it was . . . an act.

"Well." Her throat bobbed, nerves only I could recognize making her little finger twitch as she dug the nail into her thigh. "I uh, I came away with my fiancé. We wanted a bit of *us* time. We have been arranging our wedding."

My legs finally gave way, my hands snatching hold of the sofa to direct my shocked body onto it. Jenson was beside me in seconds, his arm sliding around my shoulder to comfort me. I flipped him off, pulling away from him. "Don't . . ."

"Oh!" the annoying bitch screeched on screen. "Oh, that is exciting."

The forced smile Faye gave made my gut settle. She was lying.

13

I could see it. I knew every single one of her expressions, each of her little ways and all that her body language said.

"I have seen your handsome fiancé who very much resembles your co-star and rumored lover, Cade Troy."

"They are twins."

"So, all this speculation that you are dating Cade Troy is due to the fact you're engaged to a perfect replica." The reporter cooed like she was the head bridesmaid out for the bachelorette night.

Faye twisted in her seat, her eyes never leaving the figure off camera. "They are completely different people. Nothing alike apart from features."

"So why keep Dante Troy such a secret?"

"He isn't a secret. He is a well-established professional in his own right and field. Anyone who's worth their media degree would know that if they didn't assume and actually looked into my background. I think that's enough questions for now."

"Can I just ask when the wedding will take place and where?"

"Oh," Faye shook her head quickly. "It will be a while . . ."

"A couple of weeks!" a voice said from off camera.

The TV screen exploded when I launched the remote at it. His voice, his fucking voice! How—fucking—dare—he—talk! I was going to kill him. Very slowly. Very painfully. With as much blood spill as possible. He was going to pay for this, and I would make sure it was my bare hands that did the deed.

All eyes in the room were on me when I started to snatch things and shove them into a backpack, my rage only just bubbling below the surface. They all knew what I was capable of, what my demons were capable of, and each man was perceptively quiet.

"You ready?" Frank asked. "I need to fix this bastard almost as much as you do." The dark glaze that morphed his grey eyes into slick black orbs delighted my own darkness. This man was behind me one hundred percent. He knew Faye almost as well as I did, and he was also aware of her lies.

"Oh, yeah." A shiver raced through my body. I was more than fucking ready. "Time to bring my girl home."

I ignored Jenson's narrow eyes. I knew he didn't believe Faye was being held against her will but there was nothing more blatant to me after watching that interview. The bastard was holding something against her. Terror and anguish had been ablaze in her eyes, and the way her body sat rigid was a sign of her stubborn side fighting with what she was doing.

Jenson wouldn't know these things; he didn't know her, or her quirky little ways. Frank and I, we spent time with her. We both knew her expertly. And we both loved her.

I turned to each man. "Are you sure you're all in?" They nodded.

"I'm not sure what the fuck is going on," Jenson said. "But whatever it is, I'm still in, Cade. You're my best friend, and you know I'm with you for whatever. We do this together, like everything in our lives."

I nodded, squeezing his shoulder in thanks.

"I know Dante. He'll have every available man at his disposable."

A cruel smile twisted Frank's lips. "Not to worry, I have friends meeting us at the airport."

"Friends?" Jenson asked with a lift of his brow.

Frank was ex SAS, and his friends were dangerous fuckers to say the least. He'd had his kneecap smashed during an assignment, and had then gone into security. He was the absolute best at what he did. I hired him as Faye's personal bodyguard after a stalker had sent her death threats a few years ago. Within two weeks of his placement beside her, he'd found the bastard and slit his throat. I loved the guy, not just for that, but for his loyalty and relationship with Faye. Killing a stalker may be extreme, and not the usual practice for A-List celebrities, but this man was a known sex offender and on a very dangerous path. He sent Faye photos of her in her bedroom taken mere feet away. That was as close as he would ever get and I would have killed him myself if I hadn't paid highly for others to do it for me.

"Friends," Frank confirmed, his sinister smile making my blood hum in excitement.

They all filed out of the room.

Pulling out the small photo from my wallet I gazed at her smile, my own smile forming as my eyes slid down to her perfect breasts then over her flat stomach to the teasing hand that was buried between her legs, hiding that special part of her from my view. I turned the picture in my hand and pressed my lips against the lipstick kiss my girl had painted on the back.

"I'm coming, baby," I whispered into the air as I closed my eyes and took a fortifying breath. "Get ready, because I'm gonna slice his fucking dick off for doing this to you. That's after I've gutted the bastard."

CHAPTER 3

HOPELESSNESS

Faye

"WELL, GOOD LUCK TO YOU both." Ira, the correspondent from CNN News smiled widely. I released the tension from my body with a deep exhale as Dante showed her and the camera crew to the front door. Of course, he had been the perfect gentleman in front of them; the complete opposite to who he really was. "And thank you so much for the exclusive."

"Thank you." Dante smiled. "Malik will see you to your helicopter."

Malik appeared from nowhere, as was usual for him. I didn't stay around. I needed to be away from both of them. If I'd thought Dante would go back on his threat to publish the videos, I would have sneakily gone with Ira back to the mainland, but I had no doubt he would stick to his promise.

I was trapped, both physically and emotionally. I needed time to think.

I rushed up the stairs, not even waiting until the front door was closed. My heart beat too fast with the anger surging through me, making me lightheaded and tearful. Swiping at my face, refusing to allow the tears liberation, I slammed the door to the studio behind me, quickly locking it and pocketing the key. Fuck him. I would stay in there, even throughout the thirst and hunger that would descend after a day or so. I didn't want to be there. I would rather have died than live like that.

I huddled into the corner of the room when the door handle rattled, anger turning into fear and making my body shake. I drew my knees up and clung to them, wishing they were Cade.

I needed him. I missed him so much. The tears flowed as my heart squeezed tight in my chest. .

"Cade," I whispered through the choked sobs. "Baby, I need you."

"Star!" Dante growled. "Open the door!"

I didn't answer him, my sobs too intense to allow my voice box any usage.

"Baby," he said, much more calmly. My stomach heaved with the endearment. I wasn't his *baby*. I wasn't his anything. "Open the door. We need to talk. I won't hurt you."

Yeah, right!

The door rattled again and I jumped when his fist banged against it.

"I'll give you three hours, and if you haven't opened the door then I will fucking remove it. I suggest you check your attitude before I come back. I'm warning you not to piss me off anymore."

I dropped my forehead to my knees when I heard his heavy footsteps retreat down the corridor. My heart hurt so much. All the things Dante had made me do—all the things Cade could see if Dante decided to show him. Listening to me beg to be fucked would break him. Fuck! FUCK!

There was no proof I had been manipulated with drugs, that I had lost my memory, that I'd had no idea who I was. If he showed the world, my career would be over. Cade would never get over it. The images would destroy him. In the recent years since I had fallen in love with him, he'd shown me how I should be loved, and what love should be like. His touch was demanding but gentle. His love made me dream in shades that didn't even exist.

I'll admit, in the early years, Dante had loved me like that but over time he had changed, become dark and moody, an alter ego finding its way to the surface and winning against the soft side he'd had.

But Cade, he was so gentle. He had a dark side, I knew he did, and although he sometimes brought that side of him into the bedroom, which I enjoyed, he would never have allowed that side to be seen in any other aspect of our relationship. He loved with understanding, devotion and an intensity I could feel like an entity in the air around him.

Vomit burst up my throat when I thought of his reaction to the press release. It would already be on the news; Ira informed me it was going out live.

Grabbing the waste paper basket I emptied my stomach contents, which wasn't much. My ribs hurt with the violence of my heaves, nothing but bile allowing me any release against the nausea. My heart hurt as much as my stomach, my head throbbing with the constant emotional onslaught. I now understood the saying *dying of heartbreak.* I was dying, my soul battered by the shock of the cruelty of someone I once loved.

Shaking my head, trying to expel the rampant thoughts, I walked over to the shelf and grabbed the items I needed.

A new canvas was already set up in the window. I stared out at the small building that held Dante's secrets as I mixed several hues on the palette. I knew it held more information about him, *about this,* proof to my defense, but I also knew that getting access to it again now I was aware of everything would be impossible. There was no chance of ever being alone again.

As soon as the paintbrush touched the hessian board, I relaxed. The sweep of each brush stroke calmed my heart rate, and the covering of paint on canvas quieted my raging thoughts.

I was home, on the inside anyway.

MY NECK ACHED, MY EYES blinking and widening to focus again. I stretched my back, enticing the muscles back into shape. A small smile, the first one in quite a while, broke the straight line of my lips. A tear trickled from the corner of my eye as I stared at my creation. My heart lifted slightly, appreciating the view I had crafted from memory—memories, a simple thing I had taken for granted before.

I wanted to touch it, trail my fingers across the picture but I knew I had to allow the paint to dry. The urge was overpowering.

My stomach lurched when a bang resounded on the door. Where had the last three hours gone?

"Star?"

"My name is Faye!" I spat, my lip curling at the sound of Dante's pet name.

He ignored my reprimand. "Are you going to open the door now?"

"No."

Although my whole body stiffened with fear when a huge crash rang out and the door gave way, I stood my ground, staring at Dante when he appeared in the doorframe.

He smirked, giving me a small tut. "Now we have to pay for a new door."

He walked across the room towards me, his wide, angry strides causing me to back up a little.

"I'm sure *our* budget will cater," I retorted with disgust.

His steps faltered when his eyes landed on the painting behind me. A large movement in this throat alerted me to his fury, his blazing eyes fixed on the canvas.

I chuckled bitterly. "How amusing is it that you even went out and got the same tattoos as your brother. Quite sad how jealous you always were of him."

I gritted my teeth when his hand curled around my throat, his wrath lifting my feet off the ground. I didn't struggle; I didn't give him the satisfaction.

"I would love you to end my life right now. I'd rather fuck the Devil himself than you," I choked out around his hold. "You'll be killing my baby too though, Dante."

He dropped me immediately, his eyes widening. I knew he had forgotten I was pregnant. The conflict in his eyes was clear. He wanted to hurt me but the need to protect his baby was physical in the air around us.

He leaned into me, his hot breath tickling my eyelashes and making me blink. "There's only one of us who kills their child, Star."

The air escaped me with his verbal punch. No one could ever make me ache more than I already did at my choice to terminate. I was just a girl, I had no money, and we were both going to different colleges. He had so much potential and a great opportunity he never would have taken if he knew.

I scoffed, nodding. "If this is what they would have been raised with as a father, I wouldn't wish that on anyone. I did what I thought was best."

I hissed when his palm knocked my face sideways, the thread that had been holding his need to instill pain at bay finally snapping. The sting made my ears ring and I dabbed at my lip, wiping the blood away.

Makeup covered my other bruises but the impact of this hit made my lip throb and swell. He would have to look at his damage this time.

"Hurt me all you want, Dante. But I will never love you again. It's quite fucking sorrowful that you thought kidnapping me would bring me back to you. All you had to do was come home all those years ago instead of allowing me to think you were dead."

"You knew I wasn't dead when the news got back to you that I wasn't on that fucking plane. Where were you, Star? You never even looked for me! You just laid back and opened your legs for Cade. So easy. You're a fucking whore."

I didn't retaliate. I was enjoying watching him squirm under my feistiness. The empty Star who had lost her memories was timid and nervous. However, I wasn't and I never would be.

"And why didn't you come back to *me?* Hmm?"

He smiled, a cruel twist of his lips showcasing his malicious side. "Because you were screwing my brother. Are you that fucking easy that you wanted us both in your bed? Oh forgive me, of course you are, you'd probably have us both at the same time. Once a slut, always a slut."

"Once a vindictive bastard, always a vindictive bastard. You sound like a child, Dante! Grow up!"

It was dangerous to antagonize him, but I couldn't help myself. However he always won. He always fucking won.

I closed my eyes, my heart weeping when he snatched the canvas from its easel, his evil smile fixed on me. "How beautifully you paint my brother, Star."

I clenched my fists, praying he didn't destroy the only physical image I had of Cade. My own imagination had put on canvas the reality of a person who loved me so completely.

Dante tipped his head, studying the painting. "How similar we both are. You don't see it sometimes." He sneered. "Yet you paint us both perfectly."

I snatched for it when he suddenly brought the piece down on the corner of the table. A choked sob echoed around me when he lifted it back up and smiled. "Much better."

He placed it back on the easel and tapped my cheek before walking away.

My fingers pushed at the broken canvas, trying to place the ripped parts back together and fix the gaping hole in Cade's face. Paint smudged on my fingers, the image still wet. I had never felt so much hatred in my whole life. I had loved Dante so much, so insanely that I would have done anything for him. But he would never see it that way. He would never understand because he didn't have an ounce of compassion. He was a paranoid fool, a self-obsessed man who couldn't accept things for what they were, only seeing them as a blatant hit against him. He had always been the same. He always saw things as a direct insult, even when people had tried to do him a favor or compliment him. He was insane.

I'd missed it. I'd seen his soul and I'd missed its desperate cry for help. Had I been so selfish that I had neglected what was so obvious in our years together?

No. I was just a young, inexperienced girl. One who had lived her life to give happiness to another. I'd lived for Dante. I'd tried to give him everything.

Exhaustion washed into me. Malik's shadow fell over me as he stopped in front of me holding a plate of food.

"Star, you need to eat."

My hand rose and came down against his cheek. "My name is Faye, you lying bastard. We are not friends. I don't even know you! You will not address me again. Do you understand me?"

22

His jaw flexed, his eyes closing while he swallowed. When his eyes opened they were lifeless, looking over my head and down the hall. He didn't answer; he walked around me and didn't look back. Good!

I needed to lie down. I was weak, every inch of me ached, my eyes were sore and stinging. Emotional overload had me ready to collapse.

Closing the door to my bedroom, I stripped off the clothes that didn't belong to me. He went all out in his lie. How could someone get away with this?

I made my way into the en-suite, blasting the shower as hot as my skin could stand and stepped under its torrent. I wanted to scald his dirty lies from me, to wash away my betrayals and my sins, make me unflawed, and make me good enough to have Cade's love again.

The steam cocooned me, giving me a blanket for my soul to cry into and hope it cleansed some of the pain.

Even if Cade could get past the sex with Dante, I was carrying his brother's child. What man would ever overlook that?

"You're so beautiful, Star. Even in your grief."

My insides curdled at the sound of his voice. The shower door opened and he stepped inside, naked. I tried to move around him but he stopped me, pinning me against the cold tiles, the hard plains of his body flush against my own. I hated him. How dare he touch me?

"Get off me, Dante. Now!"

"Stop acting like you don't come alive to my touch, Belle. We both know the truth. We both know how the heat of my body against yours is sending shock waves of familiar need through your system. Your pussy is swelling with want. The needy thud of the blood rushing to your clit is making juices wet your walls for my smooth entry."

That motherfucker. My body *did* awaken when he was naked against me but my hate overruled any subtle desire my whorish body might crave for.

"Dante, even rape victims can come. It's the body being overruled, not the mind. I can't control my body reacting to you but my mind," I leaned my lips to his ear, "now it's mine again, I will never succumb to you."

His throaty laugh unsettled my false confidence. "Let's test that!"

Before I could react, his knee forced its way between my thighs. His callous fingers, once welcomed, now invaded me without permission.

"Mmm, how you squeeze my fingers tells the truth you refuse to admit, Belle." He knew how to touch me to get the reactions he wanted to use against me. The tips of his fingers grazed my sweet spot, eliciting a build of pleasure.

I closed my eyes and let my mind work for me for once. I went back to a memory of when I first made love to Cade.

"Real love is sacrifice, unconditional, selfless and benevolent. Love is watching you from afar, happy in the knowledge that as long as you were happy, I would never tell you of my feelings. I would hold them inside and worship the feeling of knowing I felt true love. Love is craving your company, counting the thuds in my chest when you walk into a room because it's the only sound I can hear. Love is the electricity that ignites every nerve when you brush against me. Love is the million dragonflies taking flight inside my gut when I hear you giggle. If love was physical to touch, it would be your form. I sound like a pussy right now but it's not weak to love fiercely, it's powerful and a gift, the greatest there is and I'm grateful for loving you."

I swiped the tear away. Cade's words made my whole body melt. How did I get so lucky to earn his love?

My robe opened with a flick of my wrist, exposing my naked form. His eyes sparked with lust, glazing over with liquid fire. The shift in the room was tangible, coating our bodies in a burst of goose bumps. Heat slithered up my spine, heating my cheeks.

His tongue swiped out to moisten his lips as his eyes drew a caress over every inch of me. His steps pounded the floor as my heart pounded my ribcage. His scent fused with my own as his warm breath blew over my skin, making me shudder with anticipation.

He reached into my hair, pulling free the feather the stylist used to hold it in place. My hair fell like a waterfall over my shoulders, teasing my hard, aching nipples. The trace of the feather's soft stroke down my nose, over my lips and onto my chest made me shiver. Each movement awakened my nerve endings. My nipples cried for a harder touch but worshipped the erotic caress all at once. Need dampened between my legs and he hadn't even met my skin with his own touch yet.

The feather kissed down my navel, the warm air dispersing over the sensitive flesh from his breath following the path. My feverish body hungered for him.

A mewing sound resonated from my lips when he reached my pussy. The feather brushed softly over the small patch of short hair I groomed regularly as his lips met the tight hood of my clit, his soft kiss detonating shots of fire through my limbs. My weak knees buckled but Cade caught me, his hands gripping my hips. He pushed me back until I could support myself against the wall, then looking up at me, his lids low and heavy, he took my right leg and hooked it over his shoulder.

He looked pained, his brow pinching, his eyes closing briefly while he inhaled before reopening them to study between my open legs. Swallowing hard, he bit his bottom lip. "I always dreamed that you would one day allow me to pleasure you, share your beauty with me, but I never expected you to be this . . . this fucking perfect. Perfection isn't even the right word. You're God damn stunning."

A blush whipped up my face, heating my skin further, tiny dewdrops of sweat beading across my forehead and nose.

He licked his lips then pressed the tip of his tongue to me, giving the swollen muscle a quick flick, making me growl. He smirked as my eyes widened, the shock of my fierce lust stunning even myself, although Cade didn't look surprised.

"You taste like fucking heaven and sin. My cock is actually jealous of my mouth right now, but he'll wait." He swiped hard at my folds with the whole of his tongue, triggering another erotic snarl from me. "Because he gets the best part. He gets to feel every inch of your breath-taking pussy."

And then he devoured me. The noises he made as he consumed me were the hottest sounds I'd ever heard. My body trembled; my blood vibrated as the pleasure he demanded I take from him ripped my soul from my body and left me soaring high.

I clutched his hair as I shamelessly thrust my hips harder into his face and pulled him closer.

"Give it to me, baby. Let me taste you."

A silent scream tore from me when he slid a single finger inside me, curled it into my inner wall and bit gently on my clit. My body couldn't take it; my lungs screamed when my orgasm ripped the air from me and replaced it with an exquisite white hot bliss.

I was still high from my orgasm when he scooped me into his arms and carried me to the bed. Placing me gently down, he cupped my face and kissed the tip of my nose as he climbed over me. His hard cock throbbed against my belly. Without any more foreplay, he positioned his cock at my entrance and ran his thumb over my cheekbone.

"And now, after so, so long, I get to own you. I'm going so deep I'm going to possess your fucking soul, Faye."

My back arched when he slammed inside me, all the way to his balls, in one delicious thrust.

"Oh—fucking—Christ!" he gasped, his jaw clenching hard. He gritted his teeth. "Shit, I was fifteen the last time I came from the first thrust." He screwed his eyes shut and blew out a breath. "Don't fucking move!"

I watched his face, not daring to move. He felt so good inside me, his large cock stretching me wide, his balls laid against my ass. The look of pleasure on his face was intoxicating and I knew it would be engrained into my memory for many, many years.

"Baby," he finally whispered as he pulled out slowly, holding himself at my entrance for a moment before sliding back in little by little. He started to move, slowly pulling out and pressing back in. His eyes never left my face, his expression full of awe. The tight moans and long groans he made with every plunge were so erotic that I soon joined him. As he sped up and drove deeper, our combined noises echoed around us, our own sensual melody filling the air.

He slid one arm under my back and pulled me flush to him as he started to fuck me hard, lust and need taking over.

"You need to come, Faye. Jesus Christ, you need to come." He sounded so desperate that I slid my hand between us and started to rub at my clit.

"Slide your finger inside beside my cock. Fuck yourself at the same time as I do."

I shivered, his words pulling my climax to the edge. He rolled us slightly to the side as he pushed his little finger into my mouth. I knew

26

what he wanted so I wrapped my tongue around his finger, coating it in my spit. A wicked grin touched his lips when he knew I wanted what he was going to give me.

My orgasm started as he slipped his finger from my mouth and into my backside, pushing in deep as he forced his cock even deeper beside my finger. "Oh yeah," he whispered, "My girl likes it dirty."

"Cade!" I screamed as my soul touched heaven and I ground onto him harder, prompting his own climax. I'd never felt such intense pleasure from just a look but right then, as his eyes locked onto mine through our joint orgasm, he made love to me with both his body and his mind. . . .

"Oh God! Cade!" My screams filled the air, rebounding off the tiled walls and echoing back at us. Dante's fingers stilled inside me as my orgasm ripped through me. His palm encompassed my throat, bringing my head forward towards his lips.

"You cunt!" He spat before forcing my head back. The impact stung and spread like black ink on fabric, swallowing my consciousness.

A PRICK IN MY ARM woke me, the sharp sting jolting me from slumber. My eyes flew open. Cloudy vision showed me a female in front of me; the scent of Delia's potent perfume invaded my space. I scurried from the bed, landing in a not so graceful heap. Lifting my arm, I rubbed at the tiny bubble of blood.

"What the fuck did you inject into me?" I screeched, in fear of them stealing my mind.

"Calm down! It's only antenatal vitamins. I stitched your cut. It may scar, I don't have the best eyes at the moment." She sneered, walking around the bed to stand over me. I grinned when I saw her eyes blackened. Bitch deserved more than that.

Her eyes narrowed at my pleasure. "I'll be downstairs seeing to

Dante. If you feel nauseous, that's the sign of a healthy pregnancy."

How could I ever hope to have a healthy pregnancy when Dante couldn't go one day without inflicting injury on me? I didn't even remember leaving the shower.

"You know . . . I watch a lot of Entertainment Tonight."

And? This bitch was going to inflict pain worse than Dante could, I just knew it.

"I see Cade had been comforted by that stylist of his. Didn't take him long to move on." She smirked, leaving devastation in her wake.

Amy! I had exposed my jealousy about the over-familiar acts of Amy to Cade many times which he found hilarious; adorable was his exact word. *'She is like a little sister to me, Faye, and I promise she isn't after me.'*

Would he really move on so quickly, and with her? The images possessed my thoughts, eating away at me like a million bugs invading my body, devouring me inside-out.

I stumbled as I rose to my feet. I didn't trust that doctor as far as I could punch her. I told him to keep her away yet there she was. I was losing any say I had gained. I was becoming a prisoner again and I wouldn't stand for it. I had to have some power; it was my body.

Throwing a robe on, I marched through the house. My step faltered when I came to Dante's office and found the door ajar. I could see his desk, and upon it a very naked Delia, her ass prone in the air, her waxed bits all open and on display. A heavy hand came down on her ass cheek, startling me.

My hand came over my mouth to mask any sound. I didn't want them to know I was witnessing this. It would only fuel that whore's delight.

Malik came into view; it was him slapping her ass. I stepped closer and watched him push an object into her butt; it looked like a wine stopper but a lot bigger. An anal plug. Her answering moan told me she didn't mind. His chunky fingers then prodded at her entry. He roughly finger fucked her, adding more fingers as she begged, "More!" He was practically a puppet master; his whole giant fist nearly disappeared inside her.

"Dante . . . DANTE!" She screamed. The insane bitch. I almost smiled at her pathetic obsession with someone she clearly only got to fantasize about—until he appeared into view. He must have been watching out of my line of sight but in perfect view of the show she and Malik put on.

It hurt like a knife slicing me with the sound of his zipper opening. Everything he put me through when he had a plaything right there who would play into any sick fantasy he could conjure up. How could he be so blatant with her after making me tell the world we're engaged? Insult upon insult, salt in a very open freaking wound. I wished he would just love her and forget I existed.

"I'm going to give you what you want," he said, and patted her head like a parent praising a child.

The asshole.

She was panting, the squishing sound from Malik pounding at her made the acid in my stomach crawl up my throat like a wildfire. Gripping her hair in his hold, Dante guided her mouth to his cock.

"When Star misbehaves, I'll use you to punish her from now on." His eyes flashed up and collided with my own. Tears welled and dropped with my eyelids. I had let this man into my body. I hated myself almost as much as I hated him.

CHAPTER 4

GO TIME

Cade

"THE PILOT WON'T BE READY until the morning so we have a couple hours to kill. Try and get a hold of Blue," I told Jenson, who blanched. My eyebrow quirked.

"She flew in with the band." He shrugged sheepishly.

"She's in your hotel room right now isn't she?"

"Yep, naked." He smirked.

Usually I would have busted his balls for caving and letting her travel with the band. She kicked ass at what she did but she was still a band groupie and I didn't just mean Beneath Innocence. Blue had a killer body and rock stars succumbed to it like an addict to drugs. Jet black hair down to her ass with wild blue streaks that matched her eyes surrounded a tiny body. Her 5ft 4 frame held huge tits and an ass that could rival Kim Kardashian's. Her waist was small and her legs shapely with a tattoo that started from her toe and traveled her entire length, up the side of her calf, thigh, hip and ribs, ending at her armpit. It was a tree branch. "Upas tree" according to Jenson; it apparent-ly paralyzes the heart muscle. She was known as Blue amongst her friends and bed partners because they said her hair and eyes matched the cold in her heart. I had a lot of respect for her but not for what she did with Jenson. He was in love with her and she knew it yet still took him to bed and followed him, denying she felt the same. She had walls I didn't think anyone would ever get through but when Jenson released the song *Blue Hue* with the lyrics undeniably about her, she had the chorus tattooed into the tree tattoo on her ribs.

'I'm scratching, clawing at the surface but you're impenetrable. Your taste on my tongue, your scent on my skin but your mind you won't let me in.

Let me inside; let me see you stripped of your mask, no more don't tell, no more don't ask.

I want to swim in you but I'm drowning in the blue hue.'

"Cade, I want you to keep calm when you talk with her. She knows nothing about this shit." Rolling the tension out of my shoulders I nodded and followed him to his room.

Slipping the card key into the lock, it bleeped and opened under his push. Light from the hall flooded the darkened entry. The room smelled of sweat and sex, clothes littered the plush carpets and the sound of running water alerted us to the shower running. The door to the bathroom was ajar.

Blue's shadow cast over the bed as she stood in the open doorway. Her hair covered her tits but her bare pussy was on full display and I couldn't help but look when I saw the ink there. *'Touch me'*

The girl had character that was for sure.

Jenson rushed to cover her lack of modesty. "Baby, I'm not alone," he told her, although she was staring straight at me with a raised brow.

"Hey, Cade! You come to party?" She smirked at Jenson who growled at her.

"I need to speak to you about a system you designed for my brother."

Turning into the bathroom she called out over her shoulder. "You know my work is specific to each client, Cade. I can make you something similar but I never make two of the same designs to ensure exclusivity and unpredictability in cracking them."

31

"How did you even meet him and why have you never mentioned it before?" Jenson asked.

"I don't have to tell you who I meet and what I do for them. We actually had a mutual acquaintance." She shivered, making her junk jiggle but it wasn't from the cold. "A vile man called Hunter, into some really dark market stuff. Dante made me feel safe when I was around this Hunter guy so . . ."

The shower fall changed rhythm as she stepped into it. This was stupid. I couldn't shout to her over the noise so I pushed Jenson aside and went inside. Her hair looked like liquid ink over her skin and she grinned, probably thinking I was checking her out. She was hot, there was no denying that, but my woman couldn't be rivaled, and no tits or ass could come close to hers. I just wanted answers. She could finger fuck herself and my dick wouldn't even notice. It belonged to Faye and it longed to feel her warmth around it again.

"Blue, I need to know how to disarm it."

Her cackle echoed around the room. "No chance, Cade."

"Blue," Jenson pleaded. "This is really important. He has Faye there."

Opening the shower door she stepped out. "I know, I saw the interview."

"It's not like it seems, she doesn't want to be there," I said quickly. She studied me. I didn't waver in her silent interrogation.

"I can see when someone is lying, especially when it's to themselves. Lord knows I do it enough." Her eyes flittered to Jenson but came back to me before anyone could blink. "I know she's lying but I'm not sure to what extent. I've met Dante. He isn't the type that needs to harbor women who don't want to be there. And Cade," she stepped into my space, her tone dropping and her eyes glazing, "there's not many women apart from the ones who prefer pussy to cock that wouldn't want to be there. Dante's a freak in the sack." She bit her lip before smirking.

"For fuck's sake!" Jenson breathed.

"Fine, I'll help you but this is my reputation on the line here. No one can know I helped you."

Thank fuck. God must have been smiling down on me.

It was time to bring my girl home.

CHAPTER 5

SURPRISE

Faye

HE SMIRKED AT ME, A cruel smug smile making me want to plunge my knife into his rancid heart. I'd managed to avoid him since yesterday. His appetite had obviously been sated by Delia and her rancid mouth so he'd left me alone, but now hunger and necessity had me sharing dinner with him.

"You know what I find amusing?" I popped a morsel of meat into my mouth, struggling to push it down my throat as fury constricted every muscle.

"What's that, *darling?*" he mocked, as if we were a couple sharing dinner together after a hard day at the office. His amusement and the way his jaw moved with each chew on his steak, even the way he picked up his glass of wine and sipped at it, caused every single hair on my body to vibrate in anger.

"How you actually believe your own lies." I gave him an ultra-sweet smile when his eye twitched. "I mean, you told me you weren't *poking* Delia, yet there you were, willing to dip your dick into garbage. Oh dear, how low you've stooped!"

I braced myself, sliding my fork between my lips and clasping the meat with my teeth so he wouldn't notice my face clench with worry over my boldness.

I was in a phase where I didn't care, though. If Dante wanted to reign me with violence, whether I gave him any verbal abuse or not, he would still give it me. I had nothing to lose anymore. I'd rather have died than miss Cade with the passion I missed him with right then. The pain was too intense, too agonizing. His face was constantly in my mind, his whispered words on repeat in my head, and as much as I loved him and needed him, the constant reminder of him made my heart ache more.

"You sound jealous, *dear.*"

The hilarity of the scene wasn't lost. It was like watching a movie play out, a comedy.

"Not at all, *honey.* But I'm rather worried you may have passed something on. After all, we all know how easy she is. She's not exactly a good notch on your bedpost. Even I have standards." I slapped the table with my palm and rolled my eyes, a manic laugh escaping from me. "Oh, apparently not. I fucked you when I could have had the better half all along."

My whole body clenched when he flew across the table, his fingers clawing at my throat. I knew I had pushed him too far, but as he delved inside me with a piercing glare, he saw it—the indifference and the contempt. Gone was the timid girl; she'd died when the real Faye came back and I wouldn't allow her to control either of us again.

I knew I was up for the biggest fight of my life, but a man I had once loved so purely was strangling the life out of me and I didn't care, not one bit.

He pulled back, his glare not slipping but his grip on me disappearing. I smiled at him and then winked. "What's the matter, Dante? Can't find the woman I was before? The meek one who used to be scared of you?"

The anger he radiated was almost physical, drowning me in the thickness of his wrath, yet I held myself together, hoping my thoughts were backed up by reality; once he lost my fear he wouldn't get the same excitement anymore.

Reality was fucking beautiful. I couldn't help but smile wider when he backed up, his narrow eyes full of hatred. I had taken something from him this time; his enjoyment of hurting me.

"Pudding?" I asked as I pushed my chair back and stood up.

He didn't move. I don't think he had the ability as my disregard had stunned him but he managed to speak. "Sit down, Star. Dinner isn't over yet. We're expecting visitors."

"Oh, really, and who would that be?" I lifted his plate from the table and placed it on top of mine.

I rolled my eyes and sighed inwardly when Delia walked through the door with a huge smile on her face and a smug glint in her eye, her hips swaying over-dramatically as she sauntered across the room.

"Oh, how lovely!" I beamed at her, pulling out a chair that was set at the table between Dante and me. "Please, sit down, doctor. I was just getting dessert."

My footing stuttered when I heard the lock click. I turned to look and Dante grinned when he slid the key from the door and pocketed it.

"I'm sure cake can wait, *darling.*"

"Well, hurry, *snookums,* my sweet tooth is demanding some attention." I pulled my chair back out and settled myself into it, crossing my legs and brushing at some imaginary lint as I blew out a bored breath.

He inhaled heavily with a smile as he walked over to Delia and settled both of his hands on her shoulders. "Delia is hungry for her main course, aren't you?"

She leaned her head back and smiled up at him. I had to hold onto my laughter when she actually fluttered her eyelids.

I knew what was coming, and I readied myself, my mind going into overdrive to find something to fight back with.

Dante pulled Delia's chair back a couple of inches then slid in front of her, parking his backside on the edge of the table as he brushed an escaped tendril of hair from her face. I'd want to escape too if I was attached to *that.*

"Show Star what you want to eat, sweetheart."

Sweetheart? It was getting harder to hold the laughter in.

Her tongue swept across her bottom lip. I'm sure she thought it was sultry, but it looked a bit leery, if I was honest. She unbuckled his belt, sliding his zip down eagerly before she wrapped her talons around his shaft and pulled his already hard cock out.

Dante flicked his gaze to me, an arrogant glint lighting his eyes when Delia leaned in and ran the tip of her tongue over the slit that pooled with cum.

"You know," I said, "I'm amazed now I remember how different you taste to Cade." I pursed my lips and held a thoughtful expression.

Delia shot her puzzled eyes from Dante to me as Dante's body clenched.

"Sorry." I gave her an apologetic smile and nodded. "Carry on."

I read the confusion in both of them. Yeah, bring—it—fucking—on!

She looked up at Dante hesitantly. I hid my giggle with a cough when he gripped her hair way too tightly and directed her face back to his dick. Oh dear, he was furious. I watched how her usual puffy lips thinned when she slid him into her mouth and took his length down her throat.

"Ooh, you do it differently to me, doc. I tend to suck more. You should try it. Dante likes it that way."

I squirmed in my seat as though I was trying to get a better angle to watch her. My stomach hurt and I couldn't understand why. I hated him. He was a bastard. My throat constricted and an ache-filled lump appeared when I tried to swallow. I blinked, fighting back the feeling. I had nothing to be jealous of. Maybe I was picturing her with Cade. That was it; the ache for Cade was getting deeper and the reality that this man I once gave everything to was like a stranger. A fucked up, totally delusional stranger.

"I'm warning you, Star," Dante hissed.

I quirked a brow at him. "I'm sorry, *darling*. I thought I was helping. You must always tell her when you like something done a certain way. I mean, what was it you said about the doc? *'She reminds me of a horse'?* It's no good if those teeth get in the way, so just tell her, she can handle it."

Dante let out a growl at the same time as the lights dipped then flashed back to normal.

Delia looked up at Dante, her eyes wide and watery. He disregarded her, and dragged her back.

"I know what you're doing, Star."

I nodded and held up my hands. "I'm sorry, I'll shush now."

I straightened my back, making sure to keep my eyes fixed on Delia no matter how much it hurt me, even though I refused to accept it hurt me.

It sickened me the way she made slurping noises. Dante watched her as he guided his cock in and out of her mouth, then every now and again turned his eyes to mine. I made sure to smile encouragingly every time. I noticed she had to work hard to keep him hard. Perhaps the good doc needed the tips.

"You know, Cade has my name tattooed on his cock. That is some sexy shit. His cock always belongs to me now. And come to think of it, it's a bit thicker than yours." I held up my fingers, holding my thumb and forefinger a couple of inches apart, not stopping when he pushed Delia away and shoved his dick back into his pants. "Not much, but definitely a little bigger, although it makes all the difference . . ."

His fist in my hair yanked thousands of follicles out of my head. Dragging me across the room until I faced the end of the couch, he bent me over the arm and palmed the back of my head, driving my face into a cushion.

I struggled beneath him, regretting my stupidity. I didn't allow him to see that, though, it would have excited him even further.

"I fucking warned you. You really should listen."

Sliding a hand under my stomach, he grappled with the button on my pants as he pushed my face harder into the sofa. I became faint with the lack of oxygen. My lungs burned, but Dante seemed unaware as he yanked at the waistband of my pants, pulling them and my panties to my thighs. The action allowed me to get a lungful of oxygen when the pressure on my head gave a little.

Once again, the lights dipped but came back on and I wondered if there was a storm brewing outside. The dining room drapes had been drawn by the staff earlier when night had descended. I would have loved nothing more than to concentrate on the storm; allow it to take me some other place.

"Dante, please don't. I-"

He snatched at my hair and bent my neck back so severely it restricted the use of my voice box.

"You want this, Star. Don't deny it. I saw the way you looked at Delia. I saw the need in you. Deny it all you want but you love nothing more than when my cock is in you, filling your wet cunt or ramming the tightness of your ass."

I shook my head as much as I could, denying him the truth. I loved the connection because I had been starved of it but now he repulsed me. After the acts he committed to get me here I would never feel anything but hate for him.

"Let's see, shall we?"

I cringed when he plunged a finger into me and he laughed when he was met with a slick heat. I hated the way my body reacted to him. I hated him with a passion but my pussy evidently didn't feel the same way as it prepared for his crude entry.

Squeezing my eyes closed and fighting tears when he laughed cruelly and pushed his cock deep inside me, I prepared my mind and allowed it to take me elsewhere. My body relaxed when the memory that came to me was when Cade had taken me to the fairground . . .

"CADE!"

He laughed and, his glee at how the ride scared me shitless made me laugh too, despite the fear and my rampant heartbeat.

"Stop laughing at me!" I giggled, slapping his arm and burying my face into his chest.

"Aww, baby," he whispered in my ear as he wrapped me in his secure arms and held me tight, saving me from the view hundreds of feet in the air.

Our cage swung in the wind as the wheel came to a stop, allowing some new riders on.

"Oh my God, I don't like this," I whimpered. I was shaking, my stomach clenched as tight as my eyes.

"I bet I can make you relax." Just the way his gruff voice enveloped me eased my tight muscles.

"Oh yeah?" I murmured into his chest without opening my eyes.

"Oh yes!"

Tipping my head back with a finger under my chin, I sighed when his lips lightly brushed mine. I craved more of him. I needed him constantly; my body ached for him all the time.

He groaned when I reached for him, blindly slipping my fingers into his hair and demanding he kiss me. His mouth met mine with a sudden fury; his teeth grazing my lips as he hungrily parted them and twisted his tongue around mine, owning me and taking me. He tasted of the cotton candy and popcorn he'd wolfed down earlier, and bizarrely, it turned me on more.

He slid a hand to the nape of my neck in a tight hold as his other hand slipped under the hem of my sweater, his cold fingers splaying over my ribs and making me jump. The shock heightened my senses, turning my arousal into sheer lust. The chill on my skin reminded me of last night's play, the way he had tortured my nipples and clit with a cube of ice, and I pulled at him harder, moving one hand from his hair and cupping his hard cock through his sweatpants.

"Shit, stop, Faye or I'll tear your jeans off and take you right here, thousands of feet in the air."

I gasped, the reality of what he'd said both turning me on and driving fear through me. The clash made me shudder with need. I opened my eyes when he whispered, "Fuck, my girl likes that thought."

The heat and hunger in his eyes made me bite my lip. My pussy throbbed almost painfully. "Fear makes you hot?"

I shrugged, my cheeks blazing with embarrassment. Gripping my chin, he thrust my face to his. "Don't you dare feel shame with me. There is nothing you could say or do that wouldn't make me love you more. You wanna try bringing fear into our play, then we do that but we start gently."

I nodded, giving him a timid, grateful smile.

"Fucking hell," he whispered as he brought his mouth to mine again. "I love you."

I showed him how much I loved him as I kissed him all the way down to the bottom, our tongues twisting hungrily as our hands feverishly touched each other until . . .

I gasped, snapping out of my daydream when a loud crack fractured the air. Dante pulled out of me and moved so fast I didn't have a chance to stop myself from falling off the sofa with the sudden movement.

Everything happened so fast that I couldn't register who was stood in the broken doorway.

My hearing caught him before my sight did. My eyes landed on

39

the last thing I expected to see.

"Hello, Dante." Cade's icy voice matched the chill in his sinister grin.

I was sure my heart stopped as I passed out and gave in to the darkness.

CHAPTER 6

REVENGE AND DISAPPOINTMENT

Cade

I KNEW WITH ONE LOOK that I would kill him. My own brother, the mirror image of myself. The fury was too intense and I blew out a deep breath to take control back. My fists tightened, my knuckles cracking into place when I shifted my gaze from Faye slumped on the floor, her clothes around her knees, and back to Dante.

I couldn't breathe when I felt the familiar fog take over my senses. My bones hardened as my blood solidified, readying to protect the organs they encased as I allowed the hunger to consume me.

I hadn't relished in the destruction for years. After what happened, I never allowed it to control me anymore. But I knew, right then, I needed it.

I wanted to rush over and scoop my woman into my safe arms. I wanted the visions of her being violated by a man who wore my face, shared a womb with me, and loved once upon a time to be untrue. Nothing added up so I needed to tread carefully.

The brunette who sat at the table shot out of the chair and made for the door. I allowed her past me, knowing the guys would see to her.

I wondered why she was watching my brother rape my girl. I'd make sure she paid for that later. Apart from her, we hadn't passed another living soul on the grounds. Where was his security?

My girl moaned and shifted from her position on the floor.

"Did you hurt her?" I asked, containing the grief consuming me.

His cold stare didn't match my own, it couldn't.

"I asked you a question, Dante. Did—you—fucking—hurt—her?"

He smirked, tipping his head to the side. "You think I was raping her? Forcing myself on her?"

My chest hurt with the way I refused to allow my breathing to alter, pushing back the rage in my blood at the sight before me. Calm was the deadliest weapon and I intended to use the most lethal.

I blinked slowly when he took a step towards me and I smiled, placing my gun on the table beside me and slipping off my jacket.

"Let me tell you something, Cade," he continued walking towards me, rolling back his shirt sleeves as I flexed my hands. "Raping Star is impossible. Especially when she's more than eager to open her legs for me."

Listening to him intently, I rolled my head around my shoulders, shivering delightfully at the grind in my neck. I needed every single one of his words. I needed the fury to free my wrath. Dante wasn't aware of what I was capable of. He'd never known that side of me; the fighting in underground matches, the illegal cage fights. Nor was he aware that I had won every single one, and enjoyed it, right up until I had gone too far and killed one of my own friends.

If I had done that to a friend, he had no fucking idea what I could do to him.

I laughed, tipping my head back gleefully. "Is that right, Dante?"

He laughed with me, nodding, now stood in front of me. "Feisty little bitch, isn't she? Then again, she always was. Star likes being fucked up the ass almost as much as she enjoys my cock deep down her throat."

I leaned close, resting my mouth at his ear. "Just answer me one question. Did she call out your name or mine when she came?"

I knew he was playing me. No way would my girl let him near her unless he forced her.

I allowed him the first hit, I needed it. Every part of me came to life with the pain that shot through my face.

My body hardened, my muscles morphing into weapons that would damage him. My senses heightened, allowing me to figure out where he was going before he'd even moved. My lungs condensed, needing little oxygen to keep me fueled. The Devil himself joined my rage as I took him down.

I think he was shocked at the power I held over him. He gave back well, but he wasn't made to match my physical strength. He clearly wasn't used to being hit back, either. Prick. He would never have expected the force of my fight; the last time we'd scrapped was when we were maybe eleven or twelve and he'd floored my ass. He had made a mistake thinking it would be the same this time around.

Each spray of his blood on my skin fueled me further. Each grunt of pain that left him with the fury of my assault delighted my senses. The sound of his bones crunching made me smile and the way he lay limp and barely conscious made me laugh loud and deep. He was a tough motherfucker, no doubt about it, but he didn't have the same driving force as me, no matter how much he tried to convince himself otherwise.

I stared at him, arranged in his own blood, the red stain in the cream carpet was mesmerizing and I watched in awe as it spread out in a circle around him. Maroon 5's *Animals* played in my head, although not in context with my feelings for my brother. I couldn't help but hum along.

I stretched, cracking each joint back into place and unfolding my fingers to alleviate the pain in my knuckles as I reached for the gun.

He mumbled something I couldn't make out and I sighed in disappointment. "Do you remember when we were kids, Dante, and you took my new bow and arrow? How I swore to you that if you broke anything of mine ever again then I would kill you?" I pressed the muzzle of my gun into his temple. "Not only did you take my girl." I pressed harder. "You broke her. You broke her heart, you broke her innocence and you broke her in two by separating her from me."

He struggled to open his eyes, but when he did I hated the way they still held that victorious glint. "And I enjoyed every fucking second. She was never yours."

I closed my eyes for a second. "You're wrong. She was always meant to be mine. There was never meant to be two of us, Dante, and now there won't be."

I held his eyes, our goodbye said without words as I pressed my finger to the trigger.

"STOP!" Faye shouted. "Cade, please don't. Don't!"

I was shaking. She had pulled her clothes into place and was crawling towards me, fright so clear in her eyes it made my heart ache for her even more. I never wanted to see that look in her eyes again. She wanted to save Dante. Had he really not forced her?

"Cade, don't. I can't lose you like this," she whimpered.

Me?

"He needs to die, Faye. He deserves it."

"There are live cameras everywhere," she whispered.

"We found this motherfucker. He took Cole down," Frank spat, throwing a big guy to the ground.

"Malik! Is he breathing?" Faye asked.

"Faye!" Frank rushed over, picking her up into his embrace. I wanted her in my arms but instead I was looking down at my replica who was smirking. He must have been in agony, the sadistic prick. He was too smug for someone about to die.

"Where are the rest of your security men?"

He spat out some blood and then laughed. "Why would I need security men, you f.u.c.k.i.n.g idiot?" I pushed the muzzle of my gun into an open wound until he writhed and hissed through his teeth.

"My security system alerted the police to your presence as soon as you stepped foot on my property. They will be storming the dock within minutes."

"We're not stupid, Dante. We disabled your security system. No one is coming to save you from my bullet."

And there was the chip in his armor. I relished in his gulp.

"That's impossible." He choked on the blood filling his mouth from the busted lip.

"Yeah, Blue's pretty impressive." I grinned at him, clicking my tongue and giving him a smug wink. The flash of fear in his eyes was fleeting but I saw it.

"You just killed her," he gargled, more blood filling his throat.

"You can't kill anyone when you're no longer breathing, Dante."

The high-pitched echo of sirens filled the air, the sound faint but definitely there. What the hell?

"Smile for the fucking cameras, asshole!" The big guy laughed. Frank moved forward, swiftly kicking him in the stomach, making him cough and wheeze.

"He has cameras everywhere, Cade," Faye breathed, almost inaudibly. "There are live feeds that are nothing to do with the security system."

I jumped to my feet. "All power has been cut!"

"It works on another server to everything else, you fucking cock sucker! I'm not stupid," Dante growled.

"We need to get out of here."

"Too late."

The room swarmed with police officers screaming at me to drop my weapon. We didn't plan for police. He fucking kidnapped my girl and they were aiming their weapons at me.

I threw the gun away and raised my hands slowly, my eyes darting to Faye to make sure she was safe. The room was at a standstill. Why weren't they arresting us?

Dante struggled to his feet, wiping at the blood decorating him. "What would the public think of their famous leading man if I let them see this footage?" He smirked. Like I gave a fuck! Being an actor was a safe outlet for me; I did all my own stunts and fight scenes. It was an adrenaline rush and it made me stupidly rich. It was never to gain popularity or fans; they just came with the genes our folks gave me.

"They'd think you're a kidnapper and rapist, that's what I think."

"Is that what I am, Star?" He walked over to her. My instinct wouldn't allow me to stand and watch. I was instantly restrained by armed officers, my arms forced back in a harsh snap as I struggled in their hold.

"That's not her fucking name!" I shouted. "Just arrest us if that's your plan."

No one but Dante moved. "That's not the plan. You don't come into my house, touch me and make accusations."

"What are you going to do, kill us in front of twenty police officers?" My heart was beating out of my chest. I just wanted to get to Faye out of there. I should have shot him and left while I had the chance. I'd have risked a prison sentence if I knew she was safe and waiting for me.

"That's the difference between me and you, Cade. I was always the one with brains. I don't pay brutes to protect and serve." He walked towards me.

"Is this where your brains got you, Dante? Alone on an island where you harbor kidnapped women?"

He was grinning again. I wanted to kill him. "You've outstayed your *un*-welcome."

"I'm not leaving without her." I gritted my teeth and tried to pull from the fuckers holding me but it was useless. One shoved his gun against my spine.

"I should kill you, but a slow death is more appealing to me. One where your heart crushes you when you realize she loves me not you, and when she comes home of her own free will, I hope it fucking breaks you." He nodded to the cops holding me. They maneuvered me over to the table and pinned my hands down.

"I'll let her come with you, Cade, and every time you touch her she will feel your scars and think of me, if she isn't already."

My scars? What the fuck? The gun firing pierced the silence, followed by Faye's screams, and excruciating pain exploded in my hand before I even realized he'd shot me.

"No! You bastard, Dante. That's your brother, let him go!" Her terror was keeping me from thinking about the lava in the palm of my hand.

"It's okay, baby," I managed to get out against the shock making my body vibrate.

"Oh and, Cade, she's not your *baby.*"

Another shot rang out and my other hand ignited in pain. My vision blurred, my teeth chattering to over-ride the torture tearing through my hands.

Muffled grunts echoed around me, making me aware of my men trying to get free.

Dante held up his hand. "Get them off my fucking property, and Star . . ." He chuckled slightly and blew her a kiss. "I'll be seeing you soon . . . *baby.*"

Blood poured from my hands like a running faucet, making me queasy as I was dragged from the room with the rest of my guys, and then hit on the back of the head with a gun.

CHAPTER 7

BLOOD

Faye

THE BLOW TO THE BACK of Cade's head knocked him out cold. I had never been more lost and broken in my whole life as when he stormed that room and witnessed Dante inside me. How would he be able to look at me like he used to?

It was hard watching Cade so indulged in his demons as he held the gun to Dante. I didn't feel anything at the thought of Dante dying. I think a part of me was convinced he died long ago and the person in his place, claiming his face and name, was just a ghost wrecking the memories I had of a man I loved once upon a time.

What I couldn't face was Cade taking his life. Going to prison for the rest of his life and living with taking the life of a man he shared a womb with.

How did we get to this? Cade had a bullet hole in each palm from his own flesh and blood and it was all my fault. With every passing second he remained unconscious, a little piece of me faded with him. Jenson was restrained outside and went crazy when he saw Cade bleeding and then knocked out. I was in a dream state, my brain trying to make sense of everything.

Frank held me while my body trembled and the world washed away.

"CADE!" I SCREAMED AS I woke.

I was in a hotel. Amy was by my side, her red-rimmed eyes divulging the fact she'd been crying. What the hell was she doing there?

"Shh, it's okay, you're safe," she said, tucking some of my hair behind my ear.

"Where's Cade?"

Her eyes closed, her face contorting in pain. "He's okay. Alex is working on his hands. I can't believe his brother would do such a thing." Her timid voice showed her innocence to such violence. I kind of envied her.

Standing on wobbly legs, I pushed her hands away when they reached forward to support me. "Why are you here?"

She looked surprised by my question, her eyes popping wide making her eyebrows rise high on her forehead. "I'm here for Cade."

Yeah, the hollow black hole inside me was back, swallowing any traces of my soul. Had he moved on to her, found comfort in her? The tears sprung free, a broken dam flooding my cheeks. Death would be less painful than this. "Where is he?"

I followed her out of the room and through a corridor into another room. Cream carpets and whitewashed walls played host to the entire band, Beneath Innocence, and also Frank, Sed and Cade.

They had their trained medic, Alex, working on Cade's injuries. Alex traveled with Cade and his security. I bet he never thought he would need to fix bullet wounds.

Cade was awake and talking to Jenson. He looked pale but stunning. Every fiber in my body hummed and pulled to go to him. Silence eclipsed the sound of everyone else when his head turned to me, the only sound was my own heart stampeding in my chest.

"Faye." My name left him in a whisper.

People passed me, leaving the room, and before I could suck in a breath we were alone. He stood up wearing only his jeans that were covered in blood; his blood. God, Dante was insane. His muscled torso rippled and strained as he strode towards me. Bandaged hands grasped my face, his eyes watering, the deep brown almost obscuring his pupils.

His forehead came down to rest on mine. "I thought I'd lost you," he choked, dropping to his knees before me, his arms wrapping around my waist as his face burrowed into me. His grip was so tight it was painful. I didn't care, it made this real. He had come for me. I was with him.

My fingers swept through his thick hair, longer than Dante's. He clearly hadn't had a trim in a while. His shoulders flexed, the tattoos, half of which I designed for him, moved as if they were alive on his skin. His deep, raw scream that vibrated against my skin made my heart fracture.

He jumped to his feet and grabbed my hand, flinching from the pain in his palm. He dragged me into a bathroom and switched the shower on. "Baby, take off your clothes." He was broken, his brow furrowed and his voice cracking. I wasn't ready to do this. "Baby, you smell of him. Take your clothes off, please."

Realization hit me like a wrecking ball. He could smell the sex on me. Hurrying to rid myself of the nightmare I'd been living in I stripped the clothes away and put them in a bin in the corner of the room.

Standing under the hot spray of water, I knew it would never clean me of my sins but I was here with Cade, not Dante. The world was back in color.

Cade watched me for a while, studying every inch of me, tears slipping from his eyes every time his gaze clashed with a bruise. My throat had black and blue bruises covering it. Cade's hands were fisted, crimson rivers coating the once white bandages. That must have hurt like hell. I needed to ebb his rage.

I reached my hand out to him and waited. With each passing second he didn't move, I didn't breathe. When he slipped his hand into mine, and then his body into the small cubicle, my heart ignited. He was so selfless and forgiving; would he be if he knew it all?

"You're bleeding," I murmured, taking his palm and kissing the stains there.

"Alex numbed them."

"I'm sorry." I cried, bringing his palm to my cheek. I craved his forgiveness, his comfort, his love.

"No, don't say that. I lost you, I'm so sorry . . . he will pay for this, Faye. I promise you with my soul he will die for this."

Grabbing the soap from a shelf behind me he began cleaning my body, his touch soft like a whisper, an echo from a firmer touch I was used to. "I missed you so damn much. I missed these dimples." His hand brushed over the dimples in my lower back. He dropped to his knees, soaking his jeans and creating a red torrent with the water rinsing away the blood. "I missed this tiny scar here from when you threw an empty bottle in temper and felt so guilty when it smashed that you ran over to scoop the pieces up and kneeled on a piece." His lips kissed my knee. "I missed your unruly hair when you first wake up, the glint in your eye when you're turned on." He inhaled against my mound. My back arched and then shame made my entire body lock up. "I'm sorry, Faye. I shouldn't be touching you, I know, but I fucking died when they told me you had. I need to know you're really here. Come lay on the bed with me, please. Let me hold you."

"I need you to hold me," I whispered. "More than anything, Cade."

The sorrow in his eyes darkened and I gasped when he reached down and scooped me into his arms, water dripping a trail from the bathroom back to the bedroom where he lay me down gently on the bed and curled beside me.

CHAPTER 8

THERE IN PERSON BUT NOT IN SPIRIT

Cade

MY HEAD THROBBED, PAIN EXPLOSIVE in both palms, but her scent saturated me and faded everything else. It wasn't her pillow or her memory, it was her. Her silky strands fell in layers over my chest, her soft cheek resting on my ribs. The curves of her naked body curled around my own. She was home.

I couldn't breathe from the pure elation of having her in my arms. Nothing would ever erase how I found her. Knowing what he'd been doing to her. I wasn't prepared for the outcome I got but I should have known not to underestimate the bastard.

"He has your tattoos." Her voice was so small I was sure I'd imagined her words. Her body shifted from mine until she looked up at me. "He even has your tattoos. How did I break him so fully, Cade?"

Dante was a twisted fuck who dabbled in what he made. Even drug dealers never sampled their own product. Dante was creating his and it put him on the path of destruction. Faye didn't know I once kept

52

tabs on him. I wanted to find him when he disappeared and cut us all out of his life. When he broke her heart. I needed answers and instead found him in a volatile mood, with some whore in his bed. He didn't want to talk or listen to me. I followed him around for a week before I determined he was never like us and would never come home. If I'd known how much of a dark path his soul had gone down I would have stepped in but I wasn't a fucking saint. I had my own dark corners and questionable patches in my life; I never let any of it touch Faye, though. How could I let him do this to her, to us? I needed answers. I needed to know what he put her through and why.

"Faye, can you tell me what happened?"

Her whole frame stiffened against me. She pulled away and rushed to the bathroom, slamming the door closed. I heard the taps turn on and what sounded like whimpering.

A loud knock on the bedroom door startled me. I didn't want whoever it was to hear my girl breaking, so I wrapped the sheet around my waist and went to the door, slipping out of the room.

"Hey," Amy said, looking over me, a worried frown marring her pretty features. "How is she?"

I swallowed the scream threatening to tear me apart and shrugged my shoulders. "I've never felt this helpless before. How do I get her through this?"

"Patience." Fucking patience? I wanted to fix her now, erase every bad thing he ever did to her. Amy reached onto her tip toes, slinging her small arms around my shoulders and hugged me to her. She had been a Godsend over the last few months.

The door clicking open and then shut with an "Oh, sorry" made Amy pull away. I opened the door and found Faye in a dressing gown. "I didn't, I should have . . ."

"What, baby?"

"I didn't mean to interrupt." She shook her head and lowered her eyes to the floor.

I marched over to her, raising my hand to cup her chin. She flinched, shattering my soul. Amy's gasp brought my eyes to her. She was looking at the bruises coloring Faye's neck.

"You never have to fear me, baby." I pushed past the hurt and anger simmering under the surface of my façade. I needed vengeance.

53

"I'm sorry."

Fuck, I couldn't handle this.

"Cade." Amy said my name with caution. "This was delivered to the room, it's for Faye." She opened her palm which had a cell phone in it. I snatched it from her.

"Who the fuck delivered it?"

"Someone left it at reception. I went down to collect it. I didn't tell Frank, I came straight to you."

The phone sparked to life in my hand.

Incoming call from Dante

That motherfucker! Pressing end, my eyes went to Faye who stared at the cell like it was about to explode and kill us all. Silent seconds passed as I tried to comprehend that he knew exactly where we were and was contacting Faye like he hadn't kidnapped her at all.

Beep, beep.

Multimedia message.

The phone disappeared from my hand in a flash. Faye took off running and locked herself in the bathroom with the phone. My head felt too heavy for my shoulders; the room was spinning. Amy's hand curled around my bicep, guiding me to sit on the bed.

"I'm going to get Alex."

CHAPTER 9

UNLOVE ME

Faye

I SAW THE DESTRUCTION OF his heart flicker in his eyes as I snatched the phone from him. My own heart was about to implode. I would rather have died than let him see any video Dante had of me.

I clicked the video and muted the sound. It was of me naked and bound in red fabric. It lasted only seconds.

The phone rang in my hand and I answered it.

"I fucking hate you!"

"Keep telling yourself that, Star. You belong here with me and I'm already having withdrawal symptoms. I will give you a month! And Star . . ."

"What?"

"I know everything. You never know who is really working for me. You let him fuck you, even touch you and I'll know . . . and I'll kill him."

"You're killing *ME*, Dante. Please untouch me, unlove me, unhate me; delete it all. Erase us and let me do the same. Let me go. Please."

His bitter laugh echoed down the line, stabbing the knife already

55

burrowed in my heart further in. "I could never do that! You have my baby inside your womb. Things are how they were always supposed to be. You belong here with me and you'll come home and play your role."

"This is not a fucking game!"

"You're right about that! I only play with my prey and you, my Belle, want to be with me, want me to punish and break you down just as much as I want to do it. You crave the hunger I elicit inside you! I'm your prey and we both know it."

He was so wrong. I only craved Cade. He fulfilled everything I ever wanted and Dante had destroyed us.

"See you soon, my Belle."

The line went dead.

I caught sight of my own reflection; I couldn't bear to look at myself. Anger, grief and self-hatred bubbled to the surface. I threw the phone into the mirror, shattering it into a million pieces that could never be fixed. Just like me.

The door crashed open from the weight of Cade's shoulder ramming it. He reached for me but I stepped back, raising my hands to stop him.

"Don't touch me," I begged. Ignoring the verbal bullet killing him, Amy ushered him out and reached for me. Her soft warm hand curled around my own, pulling me from the bathroom and leading me to sit on the bed.

"You've cut your feet. I'll clean them up for you."

I didn't answer. I just stared into space, everything disappearing around me as I retreated inside myself.

I needed a little time to breathe. I believed I knew what grief was, what lonely was, heartbreak. I'd lived at the height of love, and at the bottom, and this was the most brutal pain I had ever experienced. It was like someone was sitting on my chest, sucking out my soul from the inside. I wanted to be with Cade, I wanted to be wherever he was. I wanted to marry him and bear his children, and live the life we planned but Dante took an eraser and scrubbed out that future. He wanted me and I would never be free of him. Cade would never be safe. This baby would never be safe.

"I know everything. You never know who is really working for me. You let him fuck you, even touch you and I'll know . . . and I'll kill him."

I closed my eyes to the relentless replay giving me a headache. I couldn't do this. I needed space.

CHAPTER 10

LIFE GOES ON

Cade

I COULD FEEL HIS QUESTIONING eyes on me, his pity a filthy stench around me.

"What do you want, Jenson?"

I continued to pummel the bag, relishing in the sweat that stung my eyes, each pound on the stuffed leather causing a pain to shoot through my hands and triggering a fresh outpour of blood. I needed the blood; I needed to know I could still bleed. I wasn't sure I was living anymore.

"Where is Faye, Cade?"

I winced when my teeth sank into my bottom lip and I closed my eyes for a second, catching the bag as it swung back at me. I straightened my shoulders and ran my tongue over my retreating gums. "Home."

He paused, taking a step further towards me. "No she's not. I've just come from upstairs."

I laughed, shaking my head at his stupidity. "Not my home. Hers."

"What?"

His shock matched mine when we'd flown back home and Faye had told me she needed to go back to her place. Needed space and time, she said. Still loved me, she said. Fuck, if she loved me, why did it feel so damn agonizing?

His silence was loud, his unsaid words expressive. "Cade."

"Don't!"

Ignoring him, I turned to the punch bag again, savoring the pain that overruled all other senses. I needed it to hold me up. Without the stimulant of agony I knew I would sink to my knees and let the grief consume me.

"You let her go?"

I turned on him so fast his eyes didn't have time to widen before his back hit the floor and my fingers clawed his throat, my thighs trapping his chest tightly beneath me as I leant within an inch of his face. "Tell me what I'm supposed to do, Jen. Lock her up again? Hold her here even if she doesn't wanna be here? That would make me as bad as him!"

He didn't fight me. And it wasn't because he knew he could never take me on. It was because he hurt for me. He was my best friend and he desperately wanted to take all this away from me. Just like I wanted to for him whenever life took him down.

He nodded, understanding. "But you're gonna fight," he choked out around my hold, making me realize just how tight my grip was on him. "You're gonna bring her back?"

"I can't not. I need her to breathe. To live." I closed my eyes to the sound of my own despair. I would only allow Jenson to witness it. And he was the only one who wouldn't judge me for it.

"Is she safe?"

I stared at him. "You know me better than that. Of course she's safe. I have Grant and Sed ghosting her. And she has Frank."

The door opened and we both turned. Amy's eyes widened and she slammed to a halt when she found us in what must have looked like quite a romantic moment.

"Oh my God," she screeched, backing out of the door with her eyes screwed shut. "I'm so sorry!"

Both Jenson and I stared at the door when it closed again. I couldn't hold back my own laugh when Jenson spluttered out his. "Jesus H Christ. That is one ditzy bitch!"

Our hysterics died and I lifted myself off the floor, my fingers squeezing my temples. "I need to get drunk!"

"And I know just the place." Jenson grinned as he slapped me on the back.

"YOU NEED TO BANG THAT!" I looked at Jenson through hooded eyes, pointing vaguely in the direction of the stripper flouncing her huge tits on the stage, her shaved pussy right in line with our eyes.

He nodded then sighed sadly. He was as drunk as I was. "I miss the fun we had in college, Cade. You remember that stunning Chinese girl we spit roasted. Fuck!" He held both hands up, curling his fingers into imaginary tits.

I scoffed, shaking my head and blowing out a breath at the sudden rise of nausea. Shit, I'd had way too much. "Chen!" Her name burst into my mind for some inexplicable reason. I hadn't thought of her since I was eighteen.

Jenson nodded, pointing a finger at me. "Yeah, that's her." He sighed contentedly. "Chen!"

We both shifted in our seats as visions assaulted us of that conquest many years ago. Fuck, I was horny.

"But you know, no bitch comes anywhere near Faye in the sack. Fuck, she's incredible. Knows how to move those sexy little hips she has. And Christ, when she palms her tits and rolls her fat nipples in her fingers. Makes me shiver, man. I swear she does it to torture me. She uses her pussy to get her own way."

"That's a bitch thing," Jenson slurred, trying to take a sip of his Jack but giggling like a girl when he missed his mouth and it trickled down his chin.

I nodded, agreeing with him.

"Most women want commitment. I offered that to Blue and only asked for loyalty and orgasms in return. That's all I asked for!"

"And to put it up her ass."

"Up the ass is a given in relationships." Snorting, I knocked back a shot and chased the burn with a cold mouthful of whatever the bartender filled my glass with. "Cade? It is, right? Don't be playing with me."

"I need Faye." I groaned, shifting on my stool to accommodate my hard dick. "Fuck, so bad. I haven't felt her sweet pussy in so long. I'm so hard I'm gonna knock some fucker out if I stand up."

Jenson reared back, staring at me with narrow eyes. "You need to do something about that!"

"Yeah but it's not the same. I can't even jerk myself off as good as she does it."

"Pfft," Jensen grumbled, nodding his head sadly. "Then get round there and fuck your girl!"

"I can't just turn up and fuck her."

"Why?"

"Because . . ."

"She's your fiancée, damn it! It's a given right that once you slip a diamond on her finger, her sweet little cunt should be paying you back for that rock in installments."

My head bobbed manically as my eyes followed each stab of his finger in the air with each word. "What? That's shit. I gave her a ring 'cos I want to marry her! She's my everything. I nearly lost her. Why does it feel like I still have?"

"Yes. But," he pointed to me again, the tip of his finger catching my eyeball and making me blink and squint at him, "A ring is a symbol, man. A ring for a ring."

My face screwed up in bewilderment. He'd completely ignored everything I said about the ring. "What the fuck are you on?"

"The ring. You give her a ring; she gives you her ring back! It's how it works."

"Really?"

"What the fuck, Cade? Where the hell have you been since evolution? What the hell did you think the engagement ring symbolized?"

"Well." I shrugged, grabbing onto the bar when my ass slid slightly off the stool. "Eternal love. You know, no end."

His jaw dropped as he stared at me. A bark of laughter spluttered from him. "Shit man, that's the religious ex . . . explanation." He burped loudly, rubbing his chest. "To the non-religious." His finger moved to and fro between us. "It means an eye for an eye."

"But I don't want her eye. I want between her thighs right now. I want to own her fucking heart like she does mine."

He rolled his eyes. "Freaking hell, you thick shit. It's a meteorfall."

"A what?"

"A meteorfall. You know, one of those comparison things. A sim . . . simil. . . . simile. A meteorfall!" He gave me a firm nod, this time with a bit of a wobble.

"You fucking dick, that's a metaphor!"

"Yeah. That's what I said! What the fuck is wrong with you?"

I shrugged. "I'm not drunk enough to make sense of your crap."

"My crap is serious crap, man. You know I'm right. You just hate it when you know you're not as slick as me!"

I laughed loudly, kicking my foot out and catching his leg. "How many times have I told you to stop smoking that shit?"

He smirked and I groaned when I knew what was coming. That one night at school would haunt me forever. Bastards!

"We both know who actually smokes shit!"

"Fuck off!"

He jigged about in his seat, barking loudly at me. "Your fucking face when the guys told you. You barfed your fucking guts up!"

I glared when he fell about in hysterics, his fist thumping the bar as he roared harder. "It stank, and you never freaking smelled it!"

"Fuck you!" I gagged, my mind replaying the assholes that had rolled dried dog shit and told me it was good stuff. Hell, it was my first joint, how the fuck was I supposed to know what it tasted like?

"You . . . you . . ." Tears streamed down his face as he pointed at me. "You smoked the lot. Jesus holy fuck!"

He didn't laugh when I shoved him. His body teetered backwards in slow motion, his fingers clawing the bar in a useless grip as his legs rose in the air and he tipped backwards, landing on the floor with a hefty thump, an 'oomph' bursting from his lungs.

"Now who's fucking slick?" I winked at him.

He sighed, looking up at me from the ground. "Blue left without a word again. I fucking hate her. I swear to God I'm done fucking that bitch, even if she has a magic pussy and lets me in the rear entry. Oh, and head. That woman sucks like she's getting paid to do it."

I checked my phone for the hundredth time, reading a message from Frank telling me my girl had cried herself to sleep. How did I end up here, off my face with my best friend, both of us pining for women who abandoned us?

"I'm going to fuck that stripper in the ass and tape it then send it to Blue!" Jenson announced waving her over. "You want me to buy you a lap dance?"

He should have known better than to ask that. No stripper pussy or ass wriggling up on me would do shit for me. I needed my girl. I'd give her tonight, but tomorrow if she wanted to be at her home I'd be there too.

"Hey," the stripper said. "Oh, fuck. You're the lead singer from Beneath Innocence!"

"My cock needs attention."

"Oh my God. Come into one of the private rooms and I'll take care of that for you."

Lucky prick.

CHAPTER 11

A VICIOUS CIRCLE

Faye

PULLING MY ROBE TIGHTER, I stared out of the kitchen window, appreciating the view. The poplars were thick now, their leaves a mass of green, their branches thick and powerful.

The kettle clicked off and I mindlessly filled my cup, wondering whether I could stomach milk with my coffee. After piling two heaped spoons of sugar in, I picked it up and walked out to the veranda, slowly lowering myself onto the top of the steps that led down to the garden.

Benny was doing an excellent job with the garden. It was full of color; a display of greenery and ornaments pleasing to the eye. My gaze settled on the small summerhouse at the bottom, my lips turning into a smile when I replayed some of my adventures with Cade in there.

It didn't lift my heart, though. Nothing could.

I'd spent so much time at Cade's house that my own home wasn't mine anymore. It was a building that catered for me whenever we'd had an argument. That was all it was now. Another prison that would house my heartache.

For the first time in months I'd spent a night alone in my own bed. It was large, it was cold, and it broke my heart as I'd sobbed myself to sleep.

I didn't know what to do. My eyes squeezed closed when Cade's face came swimming into my vision, his hurt and pain when I'd told him I wanted to go home. I wanted nothing more than to curl into him and stay there until my heart forgot to beat. But I knew I would never have that again.

He'd always risked so much for me. His strength had held me up time and time again. Yet it was time to find my own strength to do what was needed. To let him go.

I jolted when Frank popped his head through the door to the house. "Faye." I turned to him. "You okay?"

I sighed and lifted a brow. He nodded in understanding and came to join me, sitting beside me on the top step.

We both stared out for a while in silence, him with his coffee, me with mine. Although Frank worked for me, my 'bodyguard' as he liked to call himself, we were more like friends. He treated the house as his own and I couldn't imagine my life without him.

"I guess the two guys sat out front aren't yours."

His lips twitched before he took a sip of his drink. "No flies on you, is there?"

"Nope. Should I offer them a drink? Invite them in for breakfast?"

He shrugged. "I'm sure they're okay, it's their job. They're used to sitting in a car for hours."

"Still, it can't be nice."

Frank sighed and I shifted, swallowing the sudden lump in my throat. "We gonna talk about Cade's men all morning or are you gonna start telling me shit, lady?"

Okay, Frank had also taken on the role as father. And as much as I loved him for it, even he shouldn't be witness to what was in my head.

"You know I love you Frank." He nodded, but narrowed his eyes when I continued. "What happened between Dante and me, it stays between him and me. There is no one on this planet I would want to hurt with the truth of it all."

He pursed his lips, shaking his head slightly as his gaze remained on the garden. "That may be. But there is only you on this planet that

I hurt for."

I saw the pain in his eyes, the worry lines that had appeared across his forehead. His heart was so large but there should be no room for me in it.

Taking his hand in my own, I squeezed it as I turned back to the garden. "And there is only me who isn't worthy of it."

"That's your view," he said as he dropped my hand and snaked it around my shoulder, pulling me into him until my head rested on his shoulder. "I have some idea what happened." His body stiffened beneath me. "But you're letting him win, Faye. You're allowing him to rule you. You need to be strong now and take care of what you want. You need to put things on the table to Cade."

I closed my eyes. "But I'm trying not to hurt him by doing this."

"I know, and believe me, I understand. But Cade won't back off, Faye. You know him. He will fight the fucking Devil for you."

"That's what I'm trying to keep him from."

"Dante isn't the Devil, he's just a demon that needs to own things."

A tear dribbled off my nose and I swiped at it. "I wasn't talking about Dante," I whispered. "I was talking about me."

He paused, finally listening to me. "What do you mean?"

I pulled away, refusing to look at him. "It isn't Dante that has the capability of burning Cade. It's me, Frank. I'm the one who has the power to finish Cade. And that's why I need to push him away."

He regarded me, confusion written all over him. "Lady, I'm not . . ."

"And I'm not strong enough to explain, Frank. But you think, you all think I'm the victim in this!" I was growing angry, with myself, with Dante, even with Cade for refusing to accept what life was. "The only victim in this is Cade. The truth will crush him and I won't allow that. I'm prepared to break my own heart to free the man's that I love."

Frank stared after me as I walked away.

"DELIVERY, MISS AVERY."

"Has it been checked?"

"It has," the crackly voice came through the speaker.

"Okay, come on up." I pressed the button to the gate allowing Hanson, the designated mail guy, access to the house.

"Good morning, Miss Avery." Hanson beamed at me when I opened the door. "It's been a while since I've delivered anything here for you."

I smiled back at him, taking his clipboard and signing on the dotted line.

"Are you back for a while?" he asked over his shoulder as he walked to his van and opened the back doors.

"I'm not sure. How are Maisie and the kids?" I asked as he leaned in and pulled out a few packages.

"They're great, thank you. Sarah just got her first tooth."

I smiled widely at him but it faltered when he pulled out a huge arrangement of flowers. Sensing my nerves he pulled a face and shrugged.

"You and Mr. Troy not so . . ." His sheepish smile dropped. "Sorry, it just says the flowers came from Mr. Troy, so I presumed things weren't going so great, especially since you're back home." He lifted a hand and nodded respectfully as he handed me the bunch. "But that is none of my business. I'm sorry." He walked back to the van and pulled the door open. "Have a good day."

I nodded, giving him a smile as I went back into the house and closed the door behind me.

I couldn't help but bury my face in the enormous arrangement and inhale deeply. Gerberas, my favorite, in a variety of colors. They brought a much needed smile, although it seemed wrong, enjoying the simplicity of them. Cade had always been hyper aware of my mood and what I needed. The pure beauty of these simple flowers was it this morning.

I placed them on the dresser and pulled open the card.

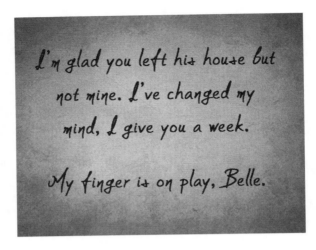

I'm glad you left his house but not mine. I've changed my mind, I give you a week.

My finger is on play, Belle.

I gritted my teeth at the rage that coursed through me. Taking the flowers, I smashed them to the floor and stomped on them like a sulky four year old, my foot crushing the delicate petals, my screams destroying what I thought they were.

"You bastard!"

I looked up to find Gina, my cleaner, staring at me with a wide mouth.

"Clean it up!" I spat. "Get rid of them. Fucking burn them!"

She continued to gawp at me as I fled up the stairs.

CHAPTER 12

NO STRANGER TO HEARTACHE

Cade

FRANK SLAPPED ME ON THE back when he opened the door and let me in. "How you doing?"

I shrugged. "Is she here?"

I could tell by the way his eyes shifted behind my shoulder that he was angry, but not with me. "She's 'busy.'" He quirked an eyebrow as he air quoted 'busy.'

I nodded, scoffing. "Oh, is she?"

He didn't stop me when I pushed past him and took the stairs two at a time. I was so fucking angry. It was time to sort this shit out.

I burst through the door to her bedroom. She was facing the window in yoga pants and a small shirt, sweat trickling down her back. She'd been working out. My teeth sank into my lip as the image of her with the weights tightened my pants.

She turned and frowned at me but carried on talking into her phone. "Well, if you think it's worth it. Of course. Who's the leading male?" She sighed, her eyes fixed on mine as she continued. "Look, Elle, I'll leave it with you. If you think it's a good role then arrange it.

Of course I'm still working and this isn't until next year, it's great to get things lined up." She stiffened, swallowing. "No, Theo isn't with us anymore so I'm promoting you." A squeal echoed from the phone making Faye cringe and me blink. "Yes, well tell them we'll look at the script."

She ended the call, her eyes staying on her phone. "New Scorsese coming up," she explained quietly.

"I don't care."

Her eyes flashed up to mine. She gulped, reading the way my body was strung. She took a step back when I took several towards her.

"You look like shit." She gasped when I closed in on her.

"I feel like shit."

She stared up at me, her striking eyes locking onto mine. I could see the mix of emotion in them; the ache, the hurt, the anguish, the devastation. I grabbed her face, my own eyes mirroring everything in hers.

"Baby, please talk to me. Don't cut me out. I won't survive that."

My forehead dropped to hers, my nose inhaling the sweet scent of her perfume and the sexy smell of her sweat.

"Cade." The word left her in a choked whisper. She lifted her hand and ran two fingers across my lips. Her eyes fluttered closed as she took a deep breath of me and slid her hands over my face and into my hair.

"I love you, Faye. Every single beautiful inch of you. I don't understand. I want to help you, take it from you." I gulped past the barricade and spoke openly, as much as it killed me to voice it. "I know . . . I know he raped you, baby." Her whimper tore my throat out. She clung to me harder. "But don't ever think that I will see you any differently because of it. Let me help you heal."

She dropped her face into my chest, a strangled cry making my heart ache. "Cade." She gripped my t-shirt in her fists, holding on like her life depended on it. "Whatever happens, you need to know that I love you so much. I'd die for you, baby." She lifted her face to look at me, tears streaking her flawless face. "I'd take the Devil's fury to stop you from hurting."

"I know that, Faye. But you don't seem to realize that I would

70

peel my own skin off for you."

A slight grimace twisted her lips. "Very graphic." She smiled. "Thank you for that."

I grinned, relishing in her smile, as small as it was. I stroked my thumb across her cheekbone, wiping her tears. "Each tear that falls from you drowns my heart a little bit more. I want to take them from you, Faye. I want to see you smile again. I want to *make* you smile again."

"I know you do, Cade. But . . . I need time."

"You can have all the time in the world. But I need you to spend that time with me. Don't push me away. Don't think I can't help, because I can. Together we can take on the world, and I know we're strong enough to get through this. You want to be here then that's fine. I'll be here too."

I took her lips, not asking but demanding. Her little moan brought my body to life. She kissed me back furiously, her hands fighting to touch me as I wrapped her ponytail in my fist and yanked her head back. The skin of her neck was soft but tinged with salt from her sweat. Unable to resist, my tongue sneaked out and tasted her, my cock throbbing appreciatively at the hit of sex on my taste buds.

My hand slid down between her breasts, the tip of my finger pressing into her as I ventured lower and rested it against her stomach.

She clammed up then pulled away, refusing to look at me. "I'm sorry." I shouldn't have pushed her, even this was progress. "I'm sorry, baby. I've just missed you so damn much." Swiping at the tears slipping from her eyes she nodded her head.

"I need to finish working out."

"Okay, I'll be downstairs with Frank, and Amy is coming to bring me a few things."

"She's sweet."

I quirked a brow at the tone of her voice, grinning internally. There was my little spitfire. She was still jealous of Amy.

AMY ARRIVED A COUPLE OF hours later, bringing pizza for everyone. Faye hadn't ventured downstairs but we were under the same roof. I could breathe easier just knowing we were in the same place.

"This was delivered today. It has *important* stamped on it and the name it was addressed to is the one you told me to always bring to your attention if any mail came." Amy faintly smiled, dropping a thick brown envelope into my lap. The addressee was a Mr. Sure. It was the name I used for the private investigator, to separate from the fan mail and scripts and shit. I flicked through all the documents inside. Theo and his girlfriend were missing and there had been no activity on either of their bank accounts. They had both fallen off the grid, a lot like my Faye.

I moved up the stairs and pressed my ear to her bedroom door, listening for movement.

"That's pervy." A dainty voice came from behind me. I spun to lay my eyes on Faye, her hair pulled back off her face, her expressive green eyes holding tinges of amber fire. Not a lick of makeup graced her face; her full red lips were begging me to taste them. Her scent encompassed me. Damn, I loved her. Her thick black lashes closed and then fluttered nervously as I quenched my thirst with her appearance.

I stumbled back, surprised when she jumped forwards, latching on to me. Her mouth crashed down on mine, her tongue angrily swiping at my own. Her supple little body pressed into mine making me come alive. I needed her so bad I could hardly function.

I turned us, kicking the door open, and then closed it once we entered her room. Her frenzied hands tore at my clothes and flesh. "We're on borrowed time, Cade. Please just love me tonight. Show me your love, our love."

The intensity of my *yes* and her desperation made everything we were doing feel like it was the last time we'd ever be together.

I wanted to tear off my bandages so I could feel her flesh beneath my palms. I would repay him for this tenfold.

I placed her down on the bed and marveled in her lust. She slipped her night shirt over her head, leaving her bare in all her perfect glory. There was a reason Hollywood wanted her as their leading lady; she was magnificent in her beauty. Her body hummed with nervous need and I would deliver what she needed, reminding her who loved her beyond any other.

I knelt before her, grasping her foot and kissing her toes, grazing my teeth over the sole of her foot and then kissing up her calf and thigh. Her foot pressed against my chest, pushing me from her. I looked down at the tear in her eye before she spun her body, pressing her tits into the bed, her ass rising up against my hard dick. "Just fuck me hard, Cade. Own me."

I stood and stripped out of my clothes, staring down at the love of my life as she pushed her face into the cushion. I loved doggy style with her. I always held her hair or throat with her head tilted up to mine so I could watch her come. This was not how we fucked. She was either trying to forget something or thinking of someone else. Did he not force her? Did she love him? Fuck, my own thoughts were sending me insane and her silence about what happened and her actions were fuelling the thoughts.

"Turn and face me, baby. I need to look at you."

Her body shook. God, I wanted her but never like this. "I can't." She hiccupped. "Forgive me Cade, please."

"Do you love him?" I had to ask, she was killing me.

"It's so complicated."

Fuck complicated! "I love you."

She turned to face me, swiping her messed up hair that had fallen from the bind holding it back. "It's weird being here. In a way I don't feel like I left there." That stung like a motherfucker. How much emotional pain can a heart withstand before it just combusts in your chest? Her words were like fire lashing at my soul, disintegrating me from the inside out. She saw him when she looked at me, and how could she not? We shared a fucking face, but not a soul, and she had always been able to make the distinction . . . or had she? Was I always just his stand in? No . . . No way, she loved me.

"Did you want to be there, Faye? Did you go to him? Fucking tell me something!"

She sat up her features scrunching up into a scowl, looking pained that I would even ask, her perfectly groomed eyebrows pulling together. "No! How could you think that?"

"You're not telling me anything! You're the other half of me, but fuck, I don't recognize you right now!"

Tears pooled in her eyes. She jumped from the bed and slapped me across the cheek, the crack loud in the quiet of the room. It stung but I deserved it.

"I was raped!"

My insides tensed, my heart exploding into an inferno of hate, despair, guilt and need for retribution. My baby went through what no woman should ever have to endure. "I'll kill him."

"He's already dead. At least I think he is."

My head spun, making the room tilt. "What?"

Her arms came around to cover her body, hugging herself. "I'm so sorry Cade. He was too strong and . . ." Her eyes were unfocused, her head shaking back and forth, lost in the memory. "I was made to shower and he came in. I hit him and he attacked me."

"Who, baby?" Tears burned my eyes.

"He didn't use his . . . his . . ." I was going to puke on her fucking carpet. I wasn't there to protect her. "He was so hateful. I never knew he hated me so much. I never did anything to him."

"Faye, who?" I whispered.

"Theo." The word left her lips like poison, spitting and sputtering. "Dante killed him." Her eyes rose to mine. I hated that Dante killed him because I would never get the pleasure. I wanted to find where Dante dumped the body just so I could see him dead for myself.

The rage inside me was going to combust and destroy everything in its wake. My fucking woman was raped! He didn't protect her. He may have killed Theo but he didn't prevent what happened to her. I wanted to reach inside her and heal her soul, take every horrible thing she suffered and burn it up, erase it and fill the space with happy memories of how loved she was.

"Did anyone else touch you?" I didn't *want* to know but needed to. I needed to know everything she went through. "Dante . . . did he force himself on you?" Guilt was written all over her. Her fingertips dug into her thigh as her tears came down in thick droplets, tainting my soul. "Do you want to be back there with him?" Did she see him as her savior from that sick fuck?

"I have to go back to him."

She might as well have taken a blade and rammed it into me. I couldn't cope; I thought we were happy before this. I thought she was over Dante, knew that what they had was an infatuation, not love like we had. She was everything to me, but why did it feel like she had died and I hadn't found her? We were over.

"You've always been the flicker in my pulse, Faye. My heart's rhythm thuds in sync with yours. We are soul mates, always were. But together the beat's becoming so fragile, baby. Loving you has been the most amazing and painful thing I have ever done. You're shutting me out, closing your heart to the memory of how it feels for me to love you. I'm losing you, I can feel it with every breath I take. We're fading and I'm dying from the loss." I took a choked breath, wincing at the pain splitting my insides in two. "So I'm setting you free to go to him. To be without me. I don't know if I'll survive losing you again but you're already gone." I lifted my hand to her head. "In here you're there with him. When I touch you," I stroked down her face with my palm, cupping her beautiful face, "is it him you feel when I kiss you?" I brought my mouth down on hers, tasting the salt from the tears cascading down her face. "Is it his love you're yearning for?" I choked on the agony crawling up my throat "You're fucking killing me, Faye. I just wish you'd use a gun."

I tore away from her feeling my soul fracture with every sob that chased my footsteps. We were done. It was a surreal moment, being witness to your own death. I'd lost her. I didn't know her anymore. She had been in his bed and wanted to be back there. She uttered my name but I knew she was fighting back his.

I wanted to yell, to lash out and say words I couldn't take back. Hold her here and force her to love me still. Force her to want only me. I was dying; this was another form of murder. How did I survive this? She threw us away. She didn't even fight for us. She didn't want to.

Her tiny footfalls chased mine, coming to a stop at the main bathroom. "Cade, wait!" She paled, her hand going to her stomach. She looked like she was holding down a retch. I reached to her stomach and she flinched, her eyes widening. My senses were alert, my head tipping to the side as I looked at her curiously. She was struggling to breathe, her face pale and clammy as her eyes shifted nervously.

"What is it?" She shook her head, still refusing to look at me. "Don't play mind games with me, Faye." I blinked, trying to think if she had a bruise on her stomach. She'd stiffened as soon as I touched her there. Why would she allow me to kiss her but not touch her belly?

Something flashed in my head. All the blood in my veins froze. My throat closed in as my heart sped up. Her gaze slowly rose to mine. Tears fell from her eyes, her face breaking when she watched me stumble backwards.

"I'm so sorry." The wail that left her splintered what was left of my damaged soul. "I . . . I . . ."

"No!" I shook my head. No, she couldn't be. No. "NO!"

She flinched when I turned and smashed my fist into the wall, bits of plaster flying when I did it again and again. "Cade! CADE!"

She grabbed for me but I moved away. "Don't! Don't fucking touch me."

"I'm sorry. I'm sorry!"

I knew it wasn't her fault, but I couldn't get past the fact that a piece of Dante was inside her. Growing in her. She was mine, yet she was pregnant with my brother's baby.

I couldn't control the insanity as it floored me and I started laughing. "Funny, isn't it?" Her tears fell harder, her sorrow as potent as the torrent of tears. "It's like we went back in time." She remained still, just watching me. "Will it be me that helps you through the termination, or will it be him?"

She lowered her eyes, confirming what I already knew. I clicked my tongue and sighed. "Neither of us. Well there's one thing, Faye." I laughed bitterly. "At least if you do decide to stay, when someone says it looks like me, they won't be wrong."

I turned when she stepped towards me and held out her hand.

"Now it's me who needs time."

"Cade, please. I'm sorry . . ."

I shook my head, gripping the door handle. "Me too, baby. Me too."

She let me go; she didn't have a choice.

CHAPTER 13

BREAKING POINT

Faye

"GOODNIGHT, FAYE," TRUDY, MY SET assistant said as she popped her head around the door.

"Night, Tru. Have a good break." She beamed at me, repeating my words back and pulling the door to my dressing room closed.

I was exhausted. Filming had run well past hours but the scene was finished and we were all eager for the few days break coming up.

The door opened slightly before Cade slipped inside, his head turned as he looked back into the corridor to make sure he hadn't been seen. "I hate all this sneaking around," he grumbled, locking the door and blowing out a breath. He was as tired as me. However, when he turned, his gaze finding mine in the mirror, his shoulders relaxed and a soft smile lit his face.

"I know, Cade. But they won't leave us alone if they find out. I can't deal with that."

He nodded, walking towards me. "It's okay, baby. I know. Fucking vultures." He was so understanding of everything I needed. I couldn't have loved him more.

"Hey." I giggled, turning in my chair to look at him properly. "Raj said to me today, 'Freaking hell, Faye. Yours and Cade's passion through the camera is explosive. The producer even commented on how real you two make it.'"

Cade laughed with me then plopped his body into my lap. A whoosh emptied from my lungs. "Oh my God, Cade, you're crushing me!"

His arms slipped around my waist and in a single move, our positions were reversed, my backside now settled on his lap. He grinned up at me. "See, told you I do all my own stunts."

I slapped his arm playfully. "Well, you need to be careful. Pete would not be happy if you injured yourself."

He smirked, waggling his eyebrows. "By the way." I shivered when his voice dropped an octave. "My tat is healed."

My eyes widened and my mouth popped open in a perfect 'O.' "So." I ran my finger across his jaw. "We're back in action?"

"Damn right we are!"

I gasped when he grabbed the edge of my robe and tore it open, finding just my underwear beneath. His face nuzzled between my breasts as a contented sigh left him. "Shit, it's been the longest ten days of my life. You do know I'm gonna last all of six seconds?"

I giggled. "Well, that's okay 'cos I'll probably only last four!"

His finger ran along the edge of my bra, tucking under the lace and seeking out my hard nipple. I squirmed in his lap when his eyes lifted to my face and he leaned forward, clamping my nipple gently in his teeth. The silk of my bra molded around me when he opened his mouth and sucked hard, pulling my flesh into the heat of his mouth. His fingers drew up my bare thigh excruciatingly slowly, the feather light touch driving me insane.

"Cade, please."

He released my nipple with a pop and stood up, my knees still tucked against his thighs. I shifted quickly, wrapping them around his waist.

The air left my lungs when he slammed my back against the wall, one of his hands supporting me as the other tore open the zipper of his pants, instantly freeing his long, hard cock.

"I'm gonna fuck you hard and I'm gonna come fast. And then

for the next five days, I'm gonna take you so slow, touch every inch of you, devour every single drop of cum you give me and you'll have no choice but to come over and over again."

I nodded. My mouth had dried up in expectation. We were spending our break in his vacation home, somewhere on the Jamaican coast. I couldn't freaking wait. It was going to be five days of nakedness and sex; lots and lots of sex.

With one quick move he had my panties in his hand and his cock buried deep inside me. Both our heads fell back as long moans of satisfaction echoed from us.

"Oh, fuck," he panted on the first thrust, "I said six but . . ."

I circled my hips, stimulating my clit on his pelvis and igniting a delicious shot of pleasure to race through me when I knew he was already teetering on the edge. The move made him growl and thrust harder, my head banging against the wall.

He fucked me harder and harder, his lust clashing with his need, driving me towards my climax faster. "Come on, baby," he growled through his clenched jaw, his eyes fixed on mine, the heat in them bringing my orgasm nearer. "Let me feel you drench my cock!"

He wrapped me in his arms then turned around and lowered me back. I seemed to hover above the ground; the only thing supporting me was his forearms. I gasped, clinging on to his strong arms as he continued to pound into me. The fear of being dropped was all I needed, my orgasm burst, my back arching so much that I could see Cade's struggle to hold onto me. But he did, and he came inside me with the fiercest of growls, his teeth bared and each vein in his neck throbbing with the pleasure raging through his system.

"Shit, shit, shit!" he hissed as he pushed hard inside me, emptying himself at the same time as he lowered us both to the floor.

I buried my face into the soft cotton of his shirt, pulling in numerous breaths as I fought to come back down. "Okay," I panted, "I thought you were going to drop me."

He laughed softly. "I'll never drop you, baby. You're too precious to drop. Besides," he whispered in my ear, "we can't break Dante's piece of pussy. Can we?"

I gasped, looking up at him. He grinned at me. It wasn't Cade anymore. This wasn't Cade. "Dante?"

I scrambled back when he laughed, the cruel tone tearing a hole through me. "NO!" I shook my head, my hands feeling behind me to find a safe route. "No!"

"Oops." Dante winked. "You gonna tell Cade or am I?"

I lunged forwards, tearing at his clothes. "No, please. You can't tell him!"

"Tell him what, Belle, how easily you come for me? How loud you scream when I fill your tight cunt? Tell him how happy you are to be growing my son or daughter inside you?"

I collapsed on the floor, struggling to breathe through the ache. "No, I don't want it. It's yours . . ."

"Ahh." He laughed again. "But you won't kill it this time, will you?"

"No," I choked out. I couldn't, not again. I had never forgiven myself for taking my baby's life, even though my head told me it had been the right thing to do. "I can't. I can't!"

"Then you know what to do!" He patted my cheek, his grin breaking my heart as he turned and walked out. "Do it, Star! Do it."

I shot upright, my heart nearly bursting through my chest as tears cascaded down my face.

"It was just a dream, Faye. Just a dream," I told myself as my hands fisted the cotton bed sheet, needing to feel something physical to confirm I was awake and Dante had gone.

I fought for control, battling with the rapid pants aching my chest as I climbed from the bed and hurried to the shower. The need to clean the sweat and tears was intense. They were tears and sweat that were shed for Dante. He didn't deserve any of my emotions.

Turning the water to the hottest point, I gritted my teeth to the pain. The tears wouldn't stop. Remembering what was growing inside me, I turned the heat down and slid down the wall, hugging my knees as I allowed the grief to consume me.

I felt sick as images of me begging Dante to fuck me slaughtered me, how he had made my body ignite for him, taken me in degrading and sick ways, ways that had me pleading for more. Cade wouldn't get through that. When he said he knew Dante had raped me, how could I tell him that was only the half-truth and that I had easily given myself to him? Now he knew, he knew I was a slut that had let his brother fuck me. I knew I had lost my memory but would Cade accept that? It seemed too farfetched to be real and the pain in his eyes when he left was everything I never wanted him to feel.

Even if I told him everything and he believed me, if Dante sent him the video footage, Cade would forever see that in his head, fracturing him inside more and more until he couldn't stand to look at me without seeing it. And when the baby came? The media would have a storm. My career would be over. I would be alone with a baby that would forever remind me of what happened and who I lost. I always thought the love we built was too strong to ever break, but I broke him.

The Dante in the dream was right. I knew what I needed to do. And I was willing to do it to save the man I loved from heartache and shame.

I slipped from the shower and rushed back to my room, avoiding Frank's eyes as I passed him where he leaned against the door frame of his room. "Amy called." I stopped walking but didn't turn. "She found Cade hammered on whiskey in his study last night. She took care of him but wants to know what happened."

I already knew she was taking care of him. I got weak and called his cell in the early hours. She answered groggily and I heard Cade groaning some shit in the background. It intensified the ice in my chest, protecting me for what was to come.

I didn't answer and made it to my room where I let out the breath burning my lungs. My eyes focused on a red dot on the white bedding. My feet carried me towards the bed, my mind hazy from witnessing blood on the sheets. My hands instinctively wrapped around my stomach. There wasn't enough blood to be a miscarriage but it could be the start of one. I had put my body through too much emotional drainage. With shaking hands I picked up the receiver and dialed.

"Hello."

"Alex, hi. It's Faye."

Silence greeted me and then some muffled sounds. "Hey Faye, are you okay?"

"I need to ask you a big favor and discretion."

The connection crackled. "Okay, but I don't like it, Faye. Cade is a good friend."

"I know and I wouldn't ask if I could go to my doctor with this."

"Of course. Do you want me to come to you?"

"Yes, and I need you to bring something. No questions or judgment."

"I'm a doctor first and foremost, Faye." He sounded offended which made me feel guilty. I was upsetting everyone lately.

More interference crackled the line. "I need a sonogram," I rushed out.

"Okay, I'll be over in a couple of hours."

I placed the phone down only for it to ring as soon as I did. I lifted it to my ear and murmured, "Hello?"

Dante's voice haunted me down the line. I slammed the receiver down over and over until it smashed apart.

My eye zeroed in on the crumbled pieces. *What the hell?* There was a recording device inside the receiver. My hands trembled as I picked it up. I knew exactly what it was. We had some installed when I had a stalker calling me all the time but that was years ago. This had to be Dante. Oh my God. Did he really have people on the inside still? Inside our trusted group? Who could I trust? What if Alex worked for him? What if he had cameras too? Oh fuck, what if he saw me with Cade?

CHAPTER 14

DRUNK

Cade

I FELT LIKE SHIT. EVERYTHING hurt, and to top it all I woke up half dressed and Amy was asleep next to me holding a sick bucket. Thankfully nothing was in it as it was knocked over.

The day passed in a haze of chugging water by the gallon and wearing sunglasses to block out the light trying to burn my retinas. The sun was too bright, voices too loud and gazes too lingering. Jenson hadn't left my side and I was grateful but also simmering with anger. Everything that left his mouth sounded condescending and I wanted to kick ass and curl up and die all in the same moment.

What did I do to deserve such a fucked up situation? I needed a plan because no matter what, Dante was going to pay for this.

The security guys holding their ear pieces and rushing out of the room gained my attention. Jenson jumped to his feet to follow them. Combined we had a shit load of men here; Jenson had upped his security because I refused to up mine.

"What the fuck's going on?" I called, slowly following behind.

"Jenson get back. Cade hold him!" Jason, Jenson's head of secu-

83

rity, bellowed.

I ran to grab Jenson but he was too fast; he bolted out of the door and down the drive. Jason shouted after him then glared back at me, making my instincts spike.

"What is it?"

"Blue." He shook his head.

I pushed past him and raced down the drive. Blue was in a heaped bundle on the ground at my gate, naked. Every inch of her skin was bruised. Blood stained her thighs and swollen face. If it wasn't for her hair and tattoos, I wouldn't know who she was.

A cry ripped from Jenson. "Oh my God. We did this."

He was right. Dante warned me and I just let it go, even when Jenson said Blue had ghosted out. She was always doing that to him so I didn't think anything of it. Pulling my shirt over my head I lay it over Blue.

"Ambulance is on its way. A van just drove up and threw her out." Jason growled. "It's a message."

All I could see when looking down at the broken and battered Blue was Faye. Did he do this to her too, or have Theo do that to her so he could act the hero and gain her love back? One thing I knew was no matter whose kid she carried or what tricks he played to manipulate her, my Faye was still in there and I would never give up on her even if she gave up on herself. I would kill Dante, but this time I'd also be prepared. I needed to find out how far his reach was and his every connection. Even if I had to get bloody to find out. The movie star Cade was gone. Hungry for revenge, the bloodthirsty Cade was in the driver's seat.

CHAPTER 15

HOME SWEET HOME

Dante

RUNNING MY TONGUE OVER MY teeth, I smiled as I terminated the call. Malik frowned, his head tipping to one side. "What's brought that smile?"

I chuckled and sighed. "Life, my friend. Life. How easily it can be controlled."

Confused by my sudden good mood he shrugged his shoulders. "I'm so glad life is good for you, but is it going the way you thought it would? Star is gone. Your brother is most probably between her legs. Your latest deal fell through, and the shit you're peddling into your body is making you ill."

Usually I would agree with him, but now? Now, none of it mattered. "Ahh, but . . ." I lifted a finger, pausing, when the doorbell rang through the house. "Right on cue."

He quirked a brow when I signaled for him to follow. I couldn't contain my grin as I slowly walked through the house with a spring in my step.

I swung the door open. The small skip in my heartbeat angered me but I ignored it and smiled. "Welcome home, *baby.*"

Malik gasped when I stepped back and she stepped inside. Her eyes were fixed on the floor, refusing to look at me. That would be the first lesson dealt with.

"Star?" Malik said in a shocked tone. She lifted her eyes to his, acknowledging him momentarily before shifting her gaze to me. She looked like shit. Her eyes were red, her face pale and gaunt.

"I'm tired." Her voice was flat. Lesson number two. "Can I go straight to my room?"

I nodded. "I'll give you that, just this once."

She nodded. "Thank you." She walked past me slowly, dragging her case.

"Malik, take Star's case up. She shouldn't be carrying anything up the stairs. After all, we need my son or daughter to be nice and healthy."

Star flinched and dropped her face back to the floor. Malik stood frozen to the spot, stunned at how easy it had been to get Star to come home.

"Malik?"

He blinked at me. "Oh yeah, sorry." He rushed forward, taking her case and following her up the stairs.

"Star!" She stopped, waiting for me to continue without turning around. "Tonight I will allow you your arrogance. But when you wake tomorrow, fresh, make sure you give me the respect I deserve."

She snorted, her head shaking slightly but didn't reply.

I watched her disappear up the stairs, my smile wider than any smile before it. How easy she was to control. Life was again how it should be. Star was mine, for good now. A baby and a wedding would make her realize she had settled for the correct brother.

After all, she had always been mine. Cade had been support for her until I reclaimed her. And how easy her support structure had crumbled. Or rather it would when he realized just where his beloved had gone. It was a shame I wouldn't be able to witness the destruction when he found out.

But never mind, just because I wasn't witness to it didn't mean it would be any less victorious. He played his hand and it was weak! The precious Blue was another message to show him I had very little morals when it came to revenge and no one was untouchable. I gave my inside man the pleasure of breaking Blue with a couple of his sadistic friends. She fucking deserved everything she got. How dare she betray me?

"How far we've come, brother." I chuckled as I made my way upstairs. "What was the pact we made when we were eleven? What's yours is mine and what's mine is my own." I laughed harder. "She was always mine." My phone buzzed in my pocket. I swiped the icon and brought my cell to my ear.

"I have the doc. I should arrive tomorrow."

"Good work. That bastard better not have harmed my baby."

"He's a pussy. He will squeal like a pig and if he doesn't, she will when she sees him."

"Good."

CHAPTER 16

THE WRATH THAT DRIVES US

Cade

I KNEW AS SOON AS I opened the door to Frank that she had gone. His eyes told me. So did the anger radiating from him. He remained silent as he moved past me.

"When?" I flinched as my voice broke and I squeezed my eyes closed to contain the desolation. I kept my back to him so he couldn't see it take me.

"Last night. I found this."

I turned to him, my eyes falling on the long cream envelope in his hand. I focused on the scrawl of my name, the 'e' smudged where one of her tears had drowned the ink.

I was struggling to hold it together, my irregular heartbeat fighting with the brisk pull of my lungs. Sweat dampened the back of my neck when I reached for the envelope. His eyes clashed with mine. "Don't pity me, Frank!"

He sighed and nodded, wisely deciding against argument, then turned and walked into the kitchen, leaving me alone as I stared at the envelope.

I pressed my thumb into the wrinkled part of paper that held her teardrop, my heart breaking with the evidence of her own heartbreak.

I heard Jenson come bounding into the apartment as I stepped into my bedroom. Slamming the door shut, warning him, I knew Frank would fill him in as I sat on the edge of the bed and opened her letter.

Cade,

I don't know how to . . . this is so hard. Before I start, you need to know that I love you, with everything, with every single breath I take. You gave me life when I didn't want to carry on, you held me up when I wanted to fall and you made my heart beat, as broken as it was. And it's only you it will ever beat for again.

But you need to know that I'm dead now, Cade. To you. Forget me.

There's much you don't know and I never want you to know. I'm not the girl you fell in love with, and that's the reason I'm doing this, to stop you from seeing the real me, the me that is so ruptured that no one, not even you will ever be able to fix. The me that you will never find it in your heart to forgive.

As much as it hurts me to say it, you need to be with someone who deserves you and the pureness of your heart. I'm tarnished and damaged now, so much so that I know the darkness in me will one day consume you, and I would never forgive myself for that. You have the biggest heart and it is worthy of a matching soul.

Although I'm not willing to say it, you know where I am. I know you don't understand why, but you don't need to, just accept this is how it is and move on with your life. But please, whatever you think of me, however much you hate me, please know that I will love you until the day my heart finally stops under the pain of losing you.

One day soon, Cade, I hope you can look through our memories and smile. Because if nothing else, the love we shared deserves that, deserves to be cherished as one that outnumbered all others on this fucking depraved planet.

I am so sorry, baby. So, so sorry.

I love you and every time my heart takes a beat you will be in my thoughts. You once told me I was the cadence in yours, well you're the cadence in mine too. It's only ever been you, Cade, but I need to go to him.

Don't come for me.

Yours forever,

Faye

I folded the paper and slipped it back in the envelope, taking out the ring she had slipped in. It was so tiny it didn't even fit onto my pinkie. It sparkled under the lights, reflecting the eyes of its owner.

It hit the mirror when I threw it, disappearing behind the dresser. The lamp on the bedside table followed it. Then the table. The pictures adorning the walls tore so easily. The spindles on the bedframe broke effortlessly in my grip. Her clothes in our wardrobe shredded like paper under my fury. The bedding that had once comforted us both ripped apart with my heart as feathers piled out onto the carpet. My screams left me as easily as the room tore apart under my heartache.

However, none of it matched the rip in my soul, the destruction of my heart or the rage that filled my veins. The obliteration of the room was nowhere near as messed up and broken as the annihilation happening inside me. Rage fueled me, anger forced my heart to beat and my wrath was the only emotion making my lungs take air. She went back to that animal.

I felt Jenson grab for me before he and Frank lifted me, both of them needing to hold me to stop my wrath as they carried me through to the bathroom and forced me into the shower. Only the sharp sting of cold water culd break the storm inside me.

Screams were the only thing that released the rage, my fists battering the tiles and smashing the ceramic as Jenson continued to grapple with me until I finally took a shuddering breath and allowed him to hold me.

My hands clawed at him as he took us to the floor and brought my body to his, his arms crushing me as he held onto me.

"Shush, buddy. Come on." His voice was choked, his devastation for me at the hands of my brother as intense as my own grief.

I cried into him until I felt the ice creep in, and the numb beat of my heart and the slow regular breaths took control. I no longer lived. I existed. My heart only beat to keep me alive. My soul died. However, I didn't need it to live. I didn't need it to seek vengeance. On Dante. And on *her* for leaving me . . . again.

She would witness a side to me she never saw before. A side I had kept from her. And now, now she deserved to not only perceive it, she deserved to witness Dante take his last breath under it.

CHAPTER 17

MANIPULATION

Faye

"GOOD MORNING!" DANTE CHIRPED WHEN I stepped in the dining room the following morning. I flicked him a glance and took the chair at the other end of the table.

He folded his newspaper precisely, placing it down beside him before standing and walking over to me. I flinched but he reached out, picking up the coffee pot and pouring the black liquid into a cup set on the table for me.

"It's a glorious sunny morning, baby. I thought we might go onto the mainland and shop. I'm sure you'll need some new toiletries and . . . personal items you didn't bring."

He added cream to my coffee and dropped in a small sugar cube.

"You need some color on your cheeks. The fresh air will do you good."

I nodded, picking up my drink and taking a sip, not really tasting it but using it to soothe my dry throat.

"We'll also find you an obstetrician. I know you're not keen on Delia, although I must say, she comes in handy."

I didn't give him the satisfaction of a reaction, knowing that was what he was pushing for.

"I've been thinking of names."

I took another sip of coffee, using it to camouflage the sharp snap of my teeth cracking under the force of my clenched jaw.

"Of course, we have to decide together, but I'm hoping we can agree." In other words, Dante had chosen a name, end of. I nodded again, picking up a piece of toast from the rack and buttering. "What are you hoping for, boy or girl?"

I shrugged, taking a bite of my breakfast and forcing myself to chew.

"Oh, by the way," he carried on, as though in the middle of an enthralling conversation. "We need to shop for a wedding dress. Three weeks today and you're all mine!" With that, he turned and walked out of the room.

The toast fell from my fingers, landing butter side down on the plate. I stared at the burnt crust. Jelly would disguise the taste. I reached across for the small pots, my head tipping left and right as I tried to decide on strawberry or redcurrant. Smiling, I dipped the spoon into the strawberry and plopped it onto the toast, then reached for the redcurrant and scooped out a portion, plopping it beside the strawberry. Taking the small jar of marmalade, I shoveled a spoonful on top of the strawberry jelly and dropped a pile of apricot jelly onto the redcurrant.

Picking up the knife, I smeared it all together, creating a rainbow of preserve that mounded high. I smiled to myself knowing Dante had gone back to his study and was watching me with a frown on his stupid, beautiful face. I couldn't decide on a flavor so why not have them all? Fuck everyone.

I took a huge bite. Then another. Only when the whole slice was devoured did I stand, place my napkin beside my plate and leave the breakfast table, passing the statue of Malik who was watching me the whole time with a raised brow.

"Cravings, what can I say?" I shrugged. Prick.

AS I WALKED INTO MY room after taking a shower, I found Dante sitting on my bed waiting for me. My fingers tightened around the top of the towel, holding it tight to me. His eyes dropped to where I was grasping tight.

"Lose it."

I fought the tremble in my legs and uncurled my fingers, fixing my gaze on the wall over his head as the towel fell to the floor. His gaze scanned me slowly, his eyes heating as he took in every contour of my body. "They say Medusa used her beauty to enslave her conquests."

I wanted to cry. But I wouldn't allow him to see my pain.

He stood from the bed and slowly strode towards me, my body stiffening with each encroaching step. He placed a finger on my chin and directed my gaze to his face. "She was the most beautiful creature that men couldn't deny. She lured them in." He leaned into me, nuzzling his nose into the skin beneath my ear. "And then, when she had them hooked." His fingers curled around my throat, his grasp harsh. "She turned them to stone." He gave me a crooked smile. "You did that to me. But instead you turned my heart to stone. So you see, Belle, it's your own beauty that made me this way."

I gulped as his palm cupped between my legs, his thumb pressing against my clit, firing me up in preparation for him. I hated the way my body came alive for him. His ability to know how to please a woman turned me on time and time again despite my mind's argument.

"Lay on the bed." His voice was a whisper in my ear, the tone low but seductive, sending a message straight to my pussy. I wanted to deny him, sew myself shut and never let him near me again but I was tainted now anyway. He could have control of my body but my mind was mine. He underestimated me.

Begging him with my eyes, he ignored me and stepped aside, tilting his chin towards the bed. I closed my mind and did as he asked.

I was tired. Tired of him, tired of fighting, tired of living this lie but it would end soon.

"Open your legs."

Again, I did as he asked, shutting down, refusing him access to my mind.

"Look at me, Star."

I moved my eyes to his face then dropped them to watch his fist enfold his erection. His cock was impressive, thick and long, the head glistening with his arousal. "You see how hard you make me, how deep my need is for you."

I flicked my eyes to his. The raw passion in them told me ownership fed his lust, and now that he owned me, his body reacted to it.

Tipping his head to the side, his eyes trailed over my nakedness, his eyelids heavy with desire and a small sigh leaving him when his gaze settled between my legs. Leaning forward, he slid his hand between my thighs and cupped me, his forefinger circling my entrance, dipping in and out occasionally.

"You see?" He smirked. "Whoever *you* think owns you, we both know the truth."

I squirmed, turning my head away from him when he slid a finger inside as he flicked my clit with his thumb, sending shockwaves of pleasure and lust through me.

It's Cade.

It's Cade.

It's Cade.

I told myself over and over. I hated that he could do that to me, make me battle my own demons to feed his. It was all a game, every single second he held control.

Instinctively, my eyes fluttered closed as my hips pressed towards the source of the pleasure, demanding more, needing more. *Cade, Cade, Cade . . .*

"That's it, Belle, open for me," he breathed as I let myself relax, my knees dropping to the side to allow him to give me what I needed. "You're like a flower, blooming and opening to feed those who need your honey. That's what you don't understand."

I started panting when he inserted another finger and fucked me harder, my hips rising as he pushed in, my chest shuddering with each stroke of his thumb over the swollen bundle of nerves ruling me. "You manipulate every man with your sweet little cunt, tempting and teasing us until we crave you with a hatred."

He twisted his hand, pressing his pinkie into my anus as he pounded into me relentlessly. I opened my eyes, giving in to the force of desire, hating myself for it as I watched his fist fluidly stroke up and down his cock, the head teasing me as his fluid dribbled over his fingers.

He groaned when he saw my eyes watching him and moved closer to me, his hands bringing both of us to orgasm. As much as I tried to hold on, I surrendered and let it go, using the bliss as an escape from a life that terrified me.

His cum sprayed over my chest, stream after stream as he groaned out my name and decorated my pale skin. His teeth clenched as his eyes locked me in his pleasure and allowed me to see his vulnerability.

He smiled cruelly, pulling his hand away from me and then wiped his fingers across my belly. He refused to release me from his stare as he moved his hand up my body, swirling his palm into his warm, sticky cum and then trailed it upwards around my neck, making me gasp.

"You wear my mark, Star." He continued to massage his seed into my skin, his hand sliding over my breasts, down my stomach and then pushing inside me. "You not only wear me, but you take me inside you. I own you now."

He moved so swiftly I didn't even have time to blink before he gripped my jaw so hard I could feel my teeth crack under the force. Dragging my face to his he sneered at me. "And don't ever forget it!"

Dropping me, he tucked himself away and left, leaving me with my tears and heartache.

CHAPTER 18

THE JEALOUS BEAST

Dante

STAR'S LAUGHTER, LIGHT AND BEAUTIFUL, flowed from the dressing room. With each step I took towards the curtained off area my stomach clenched with anticipation to see her, trying on the dress she will wear to marry me. I pulled back the curtain expecting to see her being fitted into a dress by the store clerk. What should have filled me with joy instead fired up my blood in a way I had only felt for Cade. Malik stood grinning at my Star while she giggled about God knows what; she wore only her white wedding underwear.

"What's so funny?" I barked.

Her body jolted, her hand rising to her chest. "Dante you scared me half to death. That's bad for the baby." She rubbed her stomach.

"What was so amusing?"

"I have no idea, she has baby brain or some shit she calls it." Malik continued to smile at her.

"Get dressed, Star and you! Out here."

Star's eyes widened. Malik rolled his eyes at me, the cunt. "Fine." He retreated with heavy steps.

I stalked towards Star, pushing her against the mirror. Her breath caught from the cold contact, her body laced in only her scent and two scraps of fabric covering her pride. My hand pushed on the back of her neck, my eyes questioning hers in the mirror. "What was so funny Star?"

"You making me wear white underwear." She smirked.

"Well, it was me who took your purity, so it seems fitting."

Her eyes flared. "Mmm, are you sure about that?"

Oh, she was game playing. I spun her and forced her to her knees. "I had the blood on my dick to prove it, sweet Belle, don't try those mind games with me. You'll lose! Now if you want me to treat you like a fucking dirty whore then all you have to do is ask. You know I love it when you're playing whore for me. Open up." I freed my hard cock from my slacks and nudged at her pursed lips. "Open up."

She turned her head. "No."

No? I held back my laugh. She really never learned. I yanked at the hair bundled on top of her head in a messy up-do. Her mouth opened to cry out and I shoved my dick into her, making her cry out again. She clamped down with her teeth, forcing me to snap her head back even further. Her teeth released me. "I thought we established if you bite I bite?"

Dragging her to her feet I pushed her back against the mirror. She squealed as I tore her panties from her. Her voice was muffled when I shoved them in her mouth. Her hands curled around my wrists as I lowered to my knees and used my palms to squeeze her tits spitefully, taking the focus off my mouth biting down on her mound.

She wiggled in my grasp but I was much too strong for her. I bit down enough to bruise and break the skin. I waited for the burst of metallic blood to hit my tongue before pulling away and looking up at her. "Next time you use your teeth on my dick, I'll bite your clit off."

She was completely still as the itch under my skin alerted me that I needed a fix. It left me volatile and bitter when I was due an injection. I never allowed myself to be around her when I needed a dose yet it had slipped my mind. I stood up and swiped the blood from my lips, yanking the panties from her mouth. "Oh look, I made you bleed again."

"Fuck you!" She spat in my face, her saliva hitting my cheek.

"Want to keep sharing fluids, Star? I'm down with that." I spun her again, pushing her face into the mirror. I saw no soul in my reflection. She had burned that up with her mistakes long ago and there was no retrieving it. But she would have to live with the monster she created.

I used the spit from my cheek to wet the head of my dick and then shoved up inside her, making her scream from my impolite entry. Her tits and face crashed against the glass as I pounded into her wet heat. No matter how much she told herself she hated me, her pussy loved me. Her sopping wet cunt slurped at me like a drunk on a bottle of whiskey. "Your pussy loves sucking my dick, Star."

I pulled her hair, forcing her to look at herself in the mirror. My other arm snaked around her and parted her folds. "Look at your pink throbbing clit all swollen and needy. Touch it, Belle."

"Fuck you!"

"No, sweet little slut, fuck you."

She was close; her pussy was strangling me, her face a mask of pain as she tried not to come. She didn't stand a chance. I brought my hand down hard with a slap to her pussy knowing the vibrations would ignite the simulation she needed to explode. Her inner walls drenched me in her climax, grasping my own and sucking my cum from me.

I laughed at her tears. "Such a drama queen."

I pulled my dick free and slipped my fingers inside, coating them in our mixed juices, making her pussy squelch and relishing in the burn on her cheeks from her embarrassment.

"Aww, Belle, no one's cunt gets as wet as yours. You really live for the degrading stuff."

I pulled my cell from my pocket and flicked the screen to saved images. I held up a picture of Blue before they delivered her to Cade, strung up, naked and being fucked by two guys, blood running between her legs from the abuse.

Star's eyes nearly reached her hair line, her mouth dropping open. She turned her eyes to me, water making them glimmer. She had seen the true monster I was.

"Dante." My name left her lips with barely a whisper. For whatever reason I was still a person to her before this, but from the way she was looking at me and the way my name fell from her mouth it was like she was mourning me, telling me that she had nothing left for me. It didn't matter, I didn't need her to love or want me. She had no fucking choice anymore.

"This traitor bitch didn't like being degraded but she fucking betrayed me, and Star, no one betrays me and gets away with it. Be grateful I love you."

She hiccupped on her sob. "You love me?" she said with sheer disbelief.

"You're the only person I ever loved and I hate you as much as I love you. I always will."

"For delusional reasons, Dante. You're a fucking crazy bastard! I didn't do anything to you and you're killing me for your own made up reasons."

"Enough!" I barked.

"When you cut into someone's spirit they bleed just the same as a mortal wound, it's just as deadly. You're killing me. How can you claim to love me?"

"Dante! We need to wrap it up, the store owner is getting antsy out here." Malik's voice called through the curtain.

"Get dressed." I ordered.

CHAPTER 19

GAME PLAN

Faye

I HAD ONLY BEEN BACK a week and it felt like a lifetime. I had set the wheels in motion with my plan, making sure Dante saw me laughing and touching Malik at every opportunity. I knew he had cameras everywhere and watched them like an obsessed creep. There was nothing left of the boy who once resided in his body.

The images of that poor woman. I knew her; she was a girl Jenson was in love with. Dante's damage leaked into others' lives because of me. I literally created a monster.

I was sitting on the bed when he walked in buck ass naked and sweating. He was mumbling and shaking his head in a world of his own. I stood up in shock. "Your tattoos?" I stumbled over the words. He was bare. Not any ink in sight. Fuck, was I losing my mind?

His feral eyes shot to mine. His large strides ate up the distance and I backed away, holding my hands up. He looked enraged.

"Henna ink, you stupid bitch! You think I would mark my skin permanently with that prick's ink? Are you fucking insane?"

"No, that would be you," I bravely answered, regretting it instant-

101

ly.

His pupils swallowed the whites of his eyes. He looked inhuman. "I hate you!" he spat.

"I hate you too."

"You want me to wear his ink so you can picture him fucking you while I am?"

I laughed at his bizarre actions. What was he on? "He's actually bigger than you, Dante. You don't get me off with your pencil dick. I have to pretend you're Cade to even get off." I prepared for his fury but he laughed and that was even scarier.

"Come to think of it, Star, you do feel slack down there. I'm sure we can find something to fill that hole right up." He launched at me and threw me over his shoulder. Like many times before I knew this meant I was about to be punished sexually and the worst punishment of all was making my body betray me . . . *and Cade.*

"You're hurting my stomach!" It was a cheap move but it worked. He froze and dropped me to my feet.

"I have something to show you."

"What's wrong with you? You're shaking. Dante, let me go."

He dragged me by the arm across the hall. As we passed the front door, it opened and in walked Delia flanked by Malik. The press of Dante's hold released and I fell to the ground.

"What took you so long? I'm crawling out of my skin!" he screamed at her, making her flinch. I caught her glare at me, and then she took in Dante in all his naked glory.

"I'm sorry. Come on, let's go to your office."

"Fuck that. Just give it to me now."

He was manic, his whole body vibrating. "A fucking drug addict, Dante, seriously?" I mocked.

"Shut your fucking mouth! It's because of you that I first made something to numb the pain of your betrayal."

I was sick of hearing this same shit pouring from his lips. "I didn't betray you, you stupid fuck!"

"Shut up!" he roared. His foot flew at me, colliding with my stomach. My gasp as the wind left me and Malik's voice shouting rang in my ears. Damn, I couldn't breathe. I couldn't breathe.

"Breathe, Faye." Malik's hands rubbed at my back and his voice coaxed me into taking deep breaths.

"Shit, I'm . . . I . . ."

"How could you?" I shouted, holding my stomach.

"Oh, God. Baby."

"Stop milking it, you little bitch," Delia snarled at me.

Malik lifted me from the floor and carried me to my room. "I'll get you some water," he said before leaving me on the bed.

I braced myself when Delia came into the room. "He wants me to check you over now rather than give him the medicine he needs."

I choked on a laugh, clutching the throb in my stomach. "Medicine? How can you really inject that shit into him with a clear conscience?"

She laid her briefcase on the end of the bed, entering a code and popping it open. "He needs it. You broke his heart and he began using a mix of narcotics he tweaked himself to numb you out without killing his brain cells or the dealing with a come down effect."

Was she stupid? How could she call herself a doctor? "Have you seen him? He *is* having come down effects. It's not just fatigue, you fucking idiot."

"Fuck you, you selfish little bitch. Making him feel guilty when you deserve everything you get." She pulled out a small bottle and injected a needle inside, soaking up the liquid.

"Give me your arm. I need to administer your prenatal vitamins."

"You really are as crazy as each other!" I leapt from the bed and grabbed her arm.

"Get off me, what are you doing?"

I forced her hand up, jamming the needle into her neck then pushing her away from me.

"You will never stick me with a needle again, you mental fuck." My stomach hurt from the bruise appearing there but the adrenaline pumping in my veins allowed my mind to block it out.

"Me, mental? You could have killed me!" she screamed.

"Shame I didn't. Why can't you just give him the kid he wants? Why play with people's lives like this?"

Her eyes pierced into me, her lips curling into a snarl. "You think I don't want that? He doesn't see anyone but you. He isn't interested in anyone that isn't his precious Star, and not because he loves you.

He can't love, Star. It's because you wronged him and revenge is all that drives him. He has become so used to chasing it that he doesn't even realize he destroyed you already." She laughed and it was as bitter as I felt. "Cade doesn't want you. He was seen leaving the room of that cute little assistant of his." She reveled in the pain ripping through my chest, her words verbal acid burning me through to the core. "You're damaged goods and soon enough Dante will notice that too and get rid of you."

"I'm carrying his child, Delia. He will never let me leave him." I watched to see if she would admit her sin to me. I rubbed my stomach for effect. "All you want is him and he can't even stand to put his dick in you, he uses your mouth and pretends it's mine." I tilted my head to the side, offering her fake pity.

"Fuck you!"

"He does, all the time."

Her scrawny body flew across the room, her hands tearing into my hair, her shrieks loud and ear piercing. I didn't fight her back; she played right into my hands. Seconds later Dante's voice bellowed into the room, his arms wrapping around her and throwing her to the floor.

"What the hell do you think you're doing? She's fucking pregnant, Delia!"

Oh, God how long did they think they could keep this up? "She told me I'm not pregnant Dante." I glared at him.

"What?" Delia breathed from the crumpled heap on the carpet.

His mouth opened and closed, his whole face scrunching up as a multitude of frown lines creased his forehead. "What? I saw you take the test." He looked between us both.

Delia shook her head.

"She injected me with human chorionic gonadotropin hormone to make my test positive and dupe my body into believing it was pregnant!" I accused biting out my words. "What were you going to do when I didn't get a bump or when I pushed out fucking air?"

"You're lying." He pointed his finger at me, rage still evident in his black gaze. Oh my God, was he that far gone?

"You had that doctor do something," he said.

I was beyond confused. "What doctor? She's your fucking drug supplier, Dante! Is she even a real licensed medical professional?"

He stalked towards me, gripping my upper arms. "You think I would let some cunt inject shit into you if she wasn't? Of course she is!" His eyes were unfocused. The sweat pouring from him began running down his face.

"Dante," I whispered, terrified of the beast before me. He was a drug addict, unpredictable, completely withdrawing and needing a fix.

"Alex, that little runt, was lying!"

A gasp left me. How did he know Alex? Turning abruptly he dragged me from the room, through a few corridors and out the back door. He was only wearing a towel wrapped around his waist. He walked us over to the building where I found my suitcase, the window I broke now fixed.

He keyed in a code; I watched and memorized. 10–11, my birthday. Such a simple code. We entered the room I once stood in and learned who I was but it was much too brief. We passed through door after door and down a flight of stairs, coming to a stop outside yet another door. The place was like a hospital ward, bleak with cold décor and tiled floors. It was where he had held me the first time he brought me there with no memory.

He pushed open the door and pushed me through it. I landed with a thud on the cold floor. My instincts were to bolt for the door. There was no way I could stand being locked up again. But the whimpering coming from the corner of the room stole all of my thoughts. Hair in disarray covered a man's face. Naked and huddled in the corner, his arms curled around his torso. He was filthy and bloody, clearly tortured.

"Who is this, Dante?" I broke into a small cry. Could he really be this sick?

The man inhaled sharply, his head lifting. My blood stopped flowing, solidifying in my veins. My eyes stung from the onslaught of tears, *Alex*.

"What have you done?" I crawled over to him, reaching out but too frightened to touch him. He looked sore to touch. "Alex."

"Tell me what he did, Star, or I will kill him."

"Nothing, you insane fuck!"

I held my hands up in surrender, trying to cover Alex's broken body with my own. I would rather take the brunt of Dante's anger than let him hurt another person over me again. "Dante, I asked Alex to do an ultrasound because I had a small spotting of blood. But I was never pregnant." I shook my head. His brow furrowed. "I thought you knew and were playing more games. Delia has been injecting hormones into me. Why would she do that if it wasn't a game?"

He shook his head. "Get up."

"Dante, Alex needs a doctor."

He barked out a laugh. "I'll get on that. Get the fuck up, Star!"

I rose to my feet and followed him back to the house. How the hell did he get Alex here? We collided with a sheepish Delia.

"Why?" Dante asked her with a growl.

"Because that was your end game. I wanted to speed it up."

He grabbed her by the throat. Her hands clawed at his grip. "Do you not think I would notice when no fucking baby was in there?"

"I thought . . ." She struggled to speak. Tears made her mascara run down her face like rivers of ink. "I thought you would think she aborted it."

He shoved her backwards, making her tumble to the floor, and waltzed past her.

"You thought he would get rid of me and come running to you?" I asked, astonished.

"I love him!" She screamed. "I could make him happy."

"There is no happy for Dante, Delia. He is so far gone there is no coming back for him. There is no love, no happy."

"Fuck you, you have everything!" Was she for real? I was about to retort when a loud snap shot out, ringing burst into my ears and something wet splashed over me. A scream tore from me. Delia's head had a hole in it and the missing piece decorated the floor and me. Dante stood there still in just his towel, and holding a gun.

My knees hit the floor. I couldn't breathe. I was gasping for air but nothing was coming. Did he really just do that? I hated her, but fuck, I never wanted her brain all over me. My body was going into shock. I couldn't stop the tremble rattling my spine. I was covered in her blood. I swiped maniacally at my face trying to rid the blood from me. "Get it off, get it off, get it off, get it off!" I screamed.

"WHAT THE FUCK!" came a voice I recognized. No. No. No. I wasn't seeing him. What was happening?

CHAPTER TWENTY

TRAITORS

Cade

I WAS LOSING SENSE OF time. Everything tasted the same. Liquor had no burn. Comfort had no effect. I was cold, numb. She held me up, touching cloud nine, and now she had me kissing the ground.

I crashed to it full force with no willpower to get up. Blue was in a coma and Jenson was as crushed as I was. I couldn't even answer the phone when our folks called. They kept leaving urgent messages, wanting to know what the hell was happening, but I had no answer for them.

I kept going over everything, trying to find a clue or a reason why she would write me that letter claiming I'm the love of her life yet leave me for him. Nothing made sense, but that didn't matter anymore. I needed to end him no matter what. No one I loved or had connections with was safe with Dante out there like a fucking demon beast free of its leash. I knew he was a sick fuck and way gone down the crazy train route but to let a woman be so tortured that she needed surgery to repair the tears in her anus and vagina? She may never bear children now. What kind of force did you have to use to break a woman's pelvis? Bile rose in my throat every time I pictured her lying in the hospital bed. Dislocated shoulders and a fractured jaw. Swelling on the brain. They were keeping her sedated until it was safe enough for her to wake up. Jenson cried like a little kid when the doctor listed her injuries. Police came to ask questions but no one spoke. There was no evidence to prove Dante's involvement so we would dish out our own form of justice. I needed Kenny's help. If Dante had a separate surveillance in place then it must have power and Wi-Fi to have the footage being sent somewhere.

ROLLING HIS EYES, HE WAVED me in. "Took you long enough," he grumbled. What the hell did that mean? "You won't want to see some of this shit, Cade."

I threw my jacket on the arm of his couch and pushed multiple electronic devices out of the way so I could sit down. His apartment reminded me of an old back alley collectors shop; shit everywhere. Everything looked like junk, but in fact the equipment was awesome and worth a fortune.

"I did what she asked but once I was in I decided to delve further . . . and then what happened with Blue. I want to help take this fucker down." I was stuck on the 'I did what she asked' part of his statement.

"You need to walk me through this. Who's *she?*"

He looked over the rim of his glasses at me. "Faye! She came to me."

My pulse thundered in my veins as it always did with the mention of her name. "Start from the beginning, Kenny."

"Faye came to me, walked right in on Brett and Tom going at it. She blushed like a nun at a strip joint." Like I needed to hear about his sexploits or visualize Faye walking in on him jacking off to his two boyfriends ass ramming each other.

"And?"

"She wanted me to find out where the footage went from his camera system."

"Why?"

"I don't know, she was jittering and pacing."

"Did you find out where the footage was going?"

He looked at me with a *duh* expression. "I traced them to a building built at the back of his house. This is where the power grid for all the monitors is and where they are recorded. The live feed receivers are blocked and it's taking some time breaking through firewalls and shit but I do know that everything recorded is uploaded every couple of weeks to a secure channel and stored there."

"So can you tap into the feeds?"

"Not the live feed yet but the saved footage I have."

My pulse pounded in my neck. I needed to see. "So you've seen the footage from when he took Faye?"

"I have seen some, but trust me, you don't want to see this."

"I need to."

"She begged me not to tell you I had accessed it." Why? Damn my thoughts were going to eat away at me imagining all sorts anyway. I needed to see what happened to her.

I stared at him, imploring him to understand. He walked over to his safe and unlocked it. He pulled out a packet and threw it into my lap. "My loyalty is to you, Cade, so I downloaded everything from the date of her disappearance. I warn you, it's hard to watch even for me and I'm just her friend. She also told me to tell you to look and remember the memories and smile." His hands went up when I look at him confused. "She was really specific, man, that I tell you that exactly."

"Okay, listen if I wanted to go back there, is there a way to kill the cameras?"

"It's all backed up and can only be overridden from the source. I can't delete the saved data either. It has to be done manually there. That's what she wants to do, Cade. Delete the files and shut down the cameras but I don't know her end game."

"You think she doesn't want to be there? To be with him?"

"Fuck, no! She just needs to neutralize the damage."

"She's pregnant with his kid, Kenny." I swiped my palms down my face trying to contain the despair inside me.

"Do you love her?"

"You know I do, more than anything."

"Then you bring her home and you deal with all the fallout because love is like suffocating when you're not with the person who owns it."

Damn, he was right.

"Cade, there's something else." I wasn't sure I could take much more. "I was just about to call you before you showed up. I found some interesting stuff on his server." I quirked an eyebrow. "His payroll list. All the dirty cops, all the perverted fucks he deals with. You know what that means? No cop is only dirty for one person. They care about the pay load, and we know exactly what that is and how much we need to top it, and then use the evidence I have on those fuckers to get them to turn a blind eye and let you be after it's all done."

After it's all done. He knew what I was going to have to do and would help me cover my tracks. These guys were my family, not Dante.

I CLOSED MY EYES, MY finger hovering over the play button. Kenny had warned me, and as sadistic as it sounded, I needed to see for myself. I needed to see and understand what she went through. And if it emerged that she had given herself to him freely then it was time to let her go.

An image flicked up. From the angle, it appeared that the camera was situated in the corner of a ceiling. My hand slapped over my mouth as the contents of my stomach rushed up, meeting the waste bin when I snatched it up quickly.

"Fuck!"

My eyes burned, my whole body shaking when I saw Faye, naked and dangling from a hook in the center of the grimy room. Her legs twitched as she tried to support the weight of her body, her muscles contracting tightly with her attempt to reduce the load on her arms.

Every single hair on my body snapped to attention when the lights flashed and Theo walked in with the tall guy from Dante's place. I was already struggling to hold onto my shit with the sight of him. However, I couldn't help but frown when Faye watched him warily.

The tall guy, Malik, I think his name was, un-cuffed her, catching her around the waist when she dropped. An instinctive growl curled my lip when his hands touched her bare flesh, dragging her hands around her back to re-cuff her.

My gaze landed on the bowl of bread and water on the floor but when Theo spoke to her, telling her they weren't there to serve her, I flicked to the next scene. Some things are tolerable, but watching the woman you breathe for naked, dirty and having to eat and drink from bowls on the floor like a dog, I couldn't do.

In the next scene, Faye was laid on a bed, her back to the camera as she remained completely still. She appeared to be asleep, but eventually she turned slowly, the effort of moving masking her beautiful face with pain.

She blinked, regarding something curiously.

"Hello, Star."

Dante walked into the shot. My teeth chattered against each other and I sucked my tongue to stop them grating together. I wanted to kill him. I wanted to dig my knife so far into his throat that I could feel his esophagus crack under the pressure. I wanted to watch as his blood trickled free, liberating it from its keeper, releasing his fucking soul and last breath with it.

I titled my head, straining to listen.

"Don't hurt me." Her voice was quiet; full of fear and pain.

Dante proceeded to un-cuff her then pour water down her throat. But it was their next conversation that made my eyes widen.

"Always were the defiant one."

"You . . . Do I know you?" Faye rasped as her eyes widened on him.

"What?" I choked out. This wasn't making any sense.

Dante disappeared. Faye slung the bottle across the room then my soul died when I saw her bladder empty and she sunk to the floor, screaming for them to let her out as she pounded on the door.

She didn't know him. She—did—not—recognize—Dante. What the fuck?

Numerous other scenes flashed up but I didn't stop hitting 'next' until a scene unfolded that my sick sense of need wanted to see and I hit play halfway through the scene.

"*Do you want it, Belle?*" Dante growled at her, his filthy hands holding a wand on some pearls that were barely covering Faye's pussy. She was propped up on a table by her elbows, her face tight with pleasure, and her body trembling in need. "*Tell me, do you want me inside you, fucking that throb you have building. Does your greedy little pussy want to be fed? I can smell you. Damn, I want to fuck you. Do you want me to?*"

"*Yes!*" She shouted as a sob tore up my throat. I licked at something tickling my lip, realizing it was blood when the copper tang burnt my tongue.

"*You really asking, Star? Does your pussy want to strangle my thick cock?*"

"*Damn you, Troy, just fuck me!*"

"*You asked, Star.*"

I closed my eyes when Dante freed himself and thrust inside her. Inside my girl. His filthy fucking dick taking something from her. Me.

I watched the rest of the clips in shock, my stomach emptying twice more before I couldn't watch any longer. My eyes were sore, my throat constricted with pain. My body was both weak but over-sensitized, my skin prickled with goose bumps as deep shivers ricocheted through me.

I had watched as memories came back to her, confused and twisted memories, memories Faye couldn't decipher in her own head, leading her to believe Dante was me. I had witnessed each one as they snapped inside her mind, her brow creasing, her head tipped slightly at an angle as if she tried to force the replay in her mind to make sense.

And Dante had never seen it. He'd persecuted her, degraded her and humiliated her. He'd definitely raped her, whatever stupid thoughts she had about it all. He'd played with her, manipulated her emotions until like a lost sheep she clung to the master as her only source of comfort. I understood why she had been reluctant to tell me, thinking I wouldn't believe she had lost her memories. And to be honest, maybe if I hadn't seen this footage and the way things had developed, then I would have had a hard time believing her.

The remote flew across the room as my temper snapped, hitting the wall and starting the whole damn disc to replay on fast forward, the images flicking in sequence and pouring gas onto my already burning fury.

The room took my wrath. I pulled at everything, needing to ease the raging storm inside me before it ripped me in two, my screams fuelling my rampage as the room disintegrated beneath my hands. Knick-knacks and cheap junk that Faye and I had collected over the years from our vacations that had been stored in order on a dresser scattered across the floor; the shoddy workmanship pulverized easily under my wreckage.

Finally spent, I slid down the wall, my tears dried up under my rage, my heart beating furiously as I panted, trying to bring it back into pace with my breathing.

My gaze landed on the tiny cocktail umbrella. Picking it up, I swirled it in my fingers unable to hold in the smile as the memory of that day filled my mind. I'd asked Faye to marry me a few hours earlier, and then we spent the rest of the day in our hotel room; I'd had drinks delivered. The umbrella had decorated our cocktails and I had tortured Faye with it, trailing it softly over her hypersensitive skin and tickling her until she couldn't stop the tears and the giggles.

A tear slid from my eye when I saw it was torn now, the little stick snapped in half and sharp. I snapped my eyes to the rest of the things, despair clawing its way up my throat when I realized I'd destroyed our memories.

Scooping up the fractured parts, I attempted to fix them all back together, another frantic sob bursting from me when I found them all ruined beyond repair.

"No," I whispered, gulping back the ache.

Everything was such a mess; my life as well as the souvenirs a mass of twisted and broken dreams. And she was carrying his baby. How could I ever look at it and not see him and what he did to her?

What the hell was she playing at, asking Kenny for the footage? She was up to something, I was sure of it.

'Remember the memories and smile.'

What the hell did that even mean? I picked up another trinket, sighing at the smashed Eiffel tower. I'd ruined our memories. I frowned, picking up the tiny pebble we'd found on the beach. Faye had a replica in her memory box.

In her memory box! Fuck! Her memory box!

IT WAS STILL WHERE SHE kept it on the top shelf in her closet. Lifting down the large pink box covered in a multitude of our photos that she'd glued all over it, I lifted the lid. A sharp gasp rushed from me when a blank disc in a clear sleeve lay on the top. What caught my attention, though, was the small round smiley face sticker on it.

'Remember the memories and SMILE.'

Scrambling into her bedroom, I climbed on her bed, hitting the button in the headboard that brought up the TV that was sunk into the base of her bed. It climbed slowly; too fucking slowly. As soon as it snapped into place, I slid the disc into the slot in the side and hit play.

Her image appeared on the screen.

"I hope you're watching this, Cade. I found a bug in my phone and Dante warned me he has someone in our inner circle working for him. I don't know who to trust. I hope you remember the box I kept our most precious memories in and understood my clue. Well, obviously you did or you wouldn't be looking at me now."

She giggled, the sound lighting my heart.

"People can take your soul and destroy it. They can break down your will. Break your body, your heart, but our memories are precious and the foundation of who we are. I told you when you asked if Dante raped me that it was complicated. He raped me of you, us, me, my memories. I was so lost with no connection to who I was. I woke up seeing everything in black and white and only a sadistic, lying predator to fill in the color and he did it with watercolors, blurring the images to the reality."

Her beautiful eyes filled with tears, the mass of them spilling over the edge until she swiped at them angrily and smiled sadly.

"I sensed you, though, despite it all. I sensed I was missing someone deep in the soul of me and I should have been stronger for you. I will never forgive myself for being so easily manipulated."

She sighed, lowering her eyes in shame. "God damn it, Faye! You have nothing to be ashamed of!" I shouted at the screen, angry that she wasn't real and couldn't actually hear me.

"I love you, Cade, so damn much but I need to go back to find and destroy the horrible tapes he has of me and I need to take him down so he can't ever come after you for loving me. I'm so sorry. It was all more lies and tricks, the pregnancy. I found out I'm not pregnant. He has a woman, Delia, she is a doctor. I believe she has been injecting this hormone into me. God, how screwed up is all this, Cade? How did we get here? It's all so surreal. I would give anything to be back on that beach with you slipping your ring down that thread. I know that thread is broken now. Please forgive me."

She wasn't pregnant and she was there on her own trying to take him down.

My cell trilled, making me jump. I swiped the tears soaking my cheeks and brought the phone to my ear. "Hey, man, Alex is missing."

"What?"

"And that's not all . . . Blue's awake."

"I'm on my way."

IT MADE EVERY PART OF me clench up when I passed through the doors to Blue's hospital room. I had avoided this like the plague. I felt the guilt infested in every fiber of me. I was the reason she was in there.

Her face had gone down from the swelling but the bruising painted every inch of her skin. I walked over to her bed and placed my hand down on hers. She was trembling. Tears filled her startling blue eyes. I could see the rest of Beneath Innocence sitting in the back of the room, and Jenson standing by her bedside

"I'm so sorry, Blue. He will pay with his life for this."

Her hand slipped from under mine and she slowly reached for the table that came over her bed with a piece of paper and pen resting on it. Her hand trembled as she attempted to write something down.

Frank . . . Frank . . . Frank!

"You want Frank?" What the hell, she hardly knew him.

The whole bed shook from the rattle of her tremor, her head trying to shake. I placed my hands down on her hips trying to stop her from panicking but had the opposite effect; an inhumane cry retched from her. "No . . . please!" her muffled cries called out despite her fractured jaw.

Jenson pulled me away roughly. "You can't touch her anywhere but the hand, Cade." He was torn up and I felt every ache with him. They had destroyed the woman he loved. "When I asked her who did this to her." He swiped at a few stray tears and came close with gritted teeth. "She kept writing Frank, Cade!" My vision blurred as sickness rose in my stomach. No way, Frank adored Faye. He was capable of a lot, but brutal rape? My head was buzzing, blurring out the room.

"Where the fuck is he, Cade?" I couldn't speak, memories flashed in my head from all the years Frank had worked as Faye's number one. "Where is he?" Jenson's hands fisted my shirt. He was desperate and breaking just like me.

"He said he needed to take some time off. He said he couldn't handle that Faye willingly left." I shook my head, her words echoing back at me, '*Dante warned me he has someone in our inner circle working for him.*'

I turned to single out Kenny. "On that payroll list?"

Kenny shook his head. "There was no Frank."

I closed my eyes and counted to three to stop my jaw from cracking my teeth. "What about a Jeffery Franklin Morgan?"

I knew when his pupils dilated and his shoulders stiffened.

"Fuck!" A growl ripped from Jenson's lips. "He's dead, Cade, him and Dante. We need a plan." I nodded in agreement.

Adam, the drummer for Beneath Innocence, stood from his chair and came over to us. "Look I know Cade and you used to dabble in the underground fighting scene and shit, but fuck, Jenson, we're a rock band and Cade's a movie star. We were and still are well out of our depth. Look at what they're capable of." He was scared and rightly so but he wasn't safe all the time Dante and Frank still breathed air.

"We need help," Jenson said, nodding at me.

"Who the fuck can we ask to help us kill people! Fuck, I don't know if I could even be a part of this." Adam said, pacing the floor.

"You *are* a part of this! You're one of us, and look at my woman, Adam." Jenson pointed to Blue. "I don't care what we have to do or who we have to hire to help us do it. I will do Frank myself! And I want the others who helped him. I won't rest until I make them pay."

We all startled when a man's voice boomed into the room. "I'm glad to hear that! And no hiring necessary. I will give you the men you need. I get to kill this Frank, that's my only condition." A greying man, easily six foot six stood inside the door, his expensive suit a contrast against the rugged beard and tattoos creeping up his neck.

"Who are you?"

"Daddy." A broken whisper came from Blue and then a wince and a moan of pain.

"She doesn't tell people about me and avoids me best she can. But she is my baby and those disgusting parasites have no idea whose wrath they have brought upon themselves."

CHAPTER 21

TWISTED LIES

Faye

FRANK! THE MAN WHO HAD been my bodyguard for all these years . . . he had been more than that. He was like a father to me, and all the time he was a spy for Dante. How long had Dante been planning this fucked up game of his?

Frank picked Delia up and slung her over his shoulder like she was a meat sack, blood dripping from her.

I ran back to my room, only just making it back to the toilet, and retched again. Was it Frank who had brought Alex here? How was I going to get him out of there?

"Faye!"

I bolted upright from the sound of Frank's voice, turning to peer at him standing at the bathroom door watching me. "What?"

"Thought you should know, Dante paid more. It's as simple as that. Debts need paying."

"Fuck you, Frank. I let you live in my house! I fucking cared about you!"

"I know and I still do care about you, princess. It's just business, but it doesn't mean I don't care about you, because I do."

I laughed. "Are you for real right now?" He shrugged, a blasé expression on his face. I narrowed my eyes. "Both you and Theo. Fuck. You do know what he did to me?"

His face darkened and he pursed his lips. "Yes, and he paid. Dante made sure he paid. We never wanted to hurt you, Faye, but you humiliated Dante. What the fuck did you expect him to do, smile and roll over? This is Dante, he doesn't take any shit, you know that."

My mouth fell open and I shook my head sadly. "Jesus Christ! You're all insane! Are you taking the same shit as him? We were kids for God's sake"

He sighed, rolling his eyes as if bored with me and walked away. I'd never seen this side to Frank. His betrayal hurt more than Dante's did. We'd spent holidays and vacations together with him and his wife; if it was his real wife. I wasn't sure what was real anymore. Only that I was fucked.

I refused to accept that. Dante thought I was still his timid Star, the girl he'd met in school who had bowed down to him every time, taken his mood swings and still loved him for it. Hell, I'd killed my soul when I terminated our baby, just to give him a chance at life.

It was all insane. How the hell did they expect to get away with it?

My stomach ached when I thought of Cade. I hoped he'd found the disc. I knew he wouldn't understand but I needed to tell him, to try and explain.

Pushing myself off the floor and walking back into the bedroom, I rubbed at my face. I was so tired. I ached everywhere; my head constantly pounded and my eyes were sore from so much crying.

I needed a plan. I couldn't, and wouldn't, let Dante do this to me, and to Cade. Cade didn't deserve this, he had been nothing but supportive after Dante disappeared, never overstepping the line with me until eighteen months later when neither of us could ignore our feelings. And even then we'd fought it in respect for what Dante and I had once had.

I barked out a laugh at that thought.

"You okay?"

I jumped as Malik's quiet voice came from behind me.

Turning around, I quirked a brow at him but said nothing. He stepped into my bedroom, his eyes low to the floor. "Look, Star . . ."

"My name is Faye!" I shouted at him. "Why the fuck won't anyone listen to me!"

"Faye. I just . . ." He sighed, his face tightening slightly as he closed the door behind him and walked over to me, slowly perching on the edge of my bed.

"I never thought he would go this far," he whispered, both of us aware of the cameras. "I thought he was just going to tie you up, humiliate you. I never . . ."

"Oh, come on, Malik!" I hissed, looking at him with disgust. "You allowed it to happen! You were a crucial part of this fucked up plan. You're as bad as he is!"

He nodded. "I'm not excusing myself, at all, and I'll be honest, if Dante hadn't killed Theo, I would have. I'm far from innocent." He looked at me, guilt written across his face as his hand slid over mine. "I just, I dunno, nothing has ever made me feel this conflicted before. I just want you to know that if you need a friend . . . I know life is going to be nothing but hard for you and well, well I'm here if . . ." he lowered his voice, his cheeks tinged with a red flush, " . . . if you ever need to talk or just a hug."

I couldn't hold onto my eyebrows as they shot into my hairline. Snatching my hand back I glared at him. "I needed a hug when I was hung from the hook in that room for days. I needed a hug when Dante first manipulated me and turned me against myself. I needed a hug when Dante hit me, when he abused me, when he . . . when he hurt me." I couldn't hold back the tears, the river spilling from me as I moved away from Malik when he tried to take my hand again. "Where were your hugs then, Malik?" I spat.

"I know, and I'm sorry. You have to understand, none of us got the real version of events. Dante told us you'd been with Cade behind his back for months; you'd aborted his baby because you wanted to be with Cade. I know he believed all this, but he made us believe it too, Faye."

I looked at the floor, unable to process his sudden need to repent. "Even if I fucked half the school behind his back, nothing justifies this. I didn't ever go behind his back, I loved him but we were kids." I put my hand up when he opened his mouth to reply. "I'm tired, Malik."

He nodded, pushing back off the bed and sighing again. I flinched when he bent down, his mouth resting at my ear. "For what it's worth, I truly am sorry."

He didn't say anything else but looked at me, a soft smile on his lips, then nodded and left.

I was more confused than ever. Was it a ploy? Manipulate me into thinking Malik was my friend so I would share secrets with him?

My head was splitting, too many conflicting thoughts frying my brain. I needed a distraction, and I knew just the place.

CHAPTER 22

A SIGN OF THINGS TO COME

Faye

I SMILED, A SIGH OF contentment leaving me as I leaned back and studied what my mind and hand had created, the five hours of peace and painting revitalizing me. The view from the studio window had been too good to ignore. The beautiful setting Dante's prison sat in was an artist's paradise, the sun-kissed landscape allowing use of a variety of color and textures. The gardens were absolutely beautiful and I wondered if he would allow me to venture out. Some fresh air might do me good.

One of the open windows broadcast an argument taking place. Raised male voices filtered through with the breeze. I recognized Dante's immediately. Peering out, I was annoyed that although I could hear them, they weren't clear and distinct.

Dante and Frank were squaring up to one another, Dante prodding Frank in the chest with his finger. I frowned, stepping closer to the window but it was no good; their voices were still mumbled. Frank shook his head angrily, his hands lifting as he shrugged, obviously denying something.

My eyes widened when I caught Dante flapping my panties in front of Frank, his face red with rage. What the fuck? Frank leaned further into Dante, refusing to back down to him, and once again shaking his head.

Pushing the window open as discreetly as possible I sat on the window seat and picked up a book, flicking it open to a random point, pretending to be engrossed in it.

"... Your fucking room ..." Dante shouted.

"And I'm ... you ... no idea. ... got there!" Frank growled back. "Maybe the housekeeper ... in ... wrong drawer."

Dante laughed chillingly, the sound of evil in it making me shiver. "... stupid Frank ... warning!" And with that, Dante stormed into the small outbuilding where Alex was. Frank stood mesmerized for a moment before he walked back into the house.

I was too stunned to think properly. Had Frank been through my things? Taken my underwear? I shivered with the thought of him having access to my personal belongings at home for so long. No, I couldn't believe he harbored attraction for me. He never showed anything but a parental affection towards me

And look how that turned out!

My thoughts mocked me.

Refusing to follow that crazy train in my head, I flung the book aside and decided to bite the bullet and take a walk. After all, apart from into the vast amount of ocean, there was nowhere to go.

I CLOSED MY EYES, THE sun heating my face as my lungs appreciated the fresh sea air. I had to admit the island was stunning; lengths of white sand, an open view of wave upon wave of clear blue sea. Rocks and moss-covered dunes dominated one side and to the other were vivid and flamboyant wild plants that took my breath with the array of different florae. In the middle was the impressive structure of the house sat high on the cliff.

I'd come across a small area, a waterfall cascading down the rock face that housed the house above. A pool that filtered into a thin stream leading to the ocean sat below as various garden sculptures were nestled around, most of them old, some broken and covered in ivy and other trailing plants, but all of them beautiful. A mass of untamed vegetation surrounded the scene making the whole thing tranquil and beautiful.

Sitting on a rock, I smiled for the first time in ages, my bare toes tickling the water in the pool below the waterfall as I watched an unusual bird with a diverse selection of colored feathers dip its head under the shallow part, its unwavering attempt to catch the small fish was rather entertaining.

Leaning back onto my hands slowly so as not to frighten it, I admired its determination to not give up. All of a sudden it dipped back in, pulled out a small flapping fish in its beak and took to the sky, its head held high with pride. I admired its resilience, as though giving me a message to hold on, and soon I'd fly just as high.

I shivered, an icy sensation racing up my spine when I sensed him behind me. Sighing, annoyed at his inability to leave me in peace anywhere, I turned to look at him over my shoulder. My whole frame stiffened, each hair on my body snapping to attention when I witnessed the crazy look in his eyes.

He watched me with a stare that gave me warning. He was losing his shit and because he'd just killed his administrator, he wasn't coping.

His eyes locked me down, refusing me to move as he walked towards me. I knew better than to look away, giving him the attention he was looking for. My whole body trembled in fright; the way his jaw vibrated showed me that cold turkey was not suiting him.

He stepped into the pool, the water rising up his body the further he came towards me. I braced the rock I was sat on with my hands, digging my fingers into it like it would help me. He kept moving until he was stood in front of me, the water up to his knees, his furious face moving in close to mine.

He slid his hand into his pocket and pulled out a pair of my black lace panties. "Want to know where I found these?" His voice was tight, his lungs struggling to work properly under his rage. I didn't answer him but continued to hold his secure gaze. Tipping his head, he narrowed his eyes on me. "In Frank's bedroom."

My eyes widened. Although no surprise, I needed to hide the fact that I knew.

"Why were they in Frank's possession, Star?"

"I have no idea, Dante."

I was struggling to hold on. His narrow eyes thinned further, my lie blatant to him. I gasped when his hand wrapped around my face, his long fingers digging into my cheeks. "Don't lie to me, Star. I could always see your lies."

"I don't know, Dante," I said around the force holding my jaw. I wasn't really lying, I hadn't a clue why Frank had them, but it hadn't been of any surprise, and that's what Dante saw in my expression.

His teeth clenched as he rapidly inhaled air noisily through his nose. His pupils were huge, his face twitching and his skin pale and clammy as he growled.

I tried to scramble away when he stuffed my panties into my mouth, pushing them further and further in with his finger as I choked around them. Grabbing a fistful of my hair he dragged me off the rock and plunged me into the water, his other hand pushing my head down until my face was below the surface.

Unable to fill my lungs properly due to my gag, they started screaming at the sudden disappearance of oxygen. Kicking and flaying under his strict grasp, I panicked, my head shaking as I brought my fingers up to grab hold of his wrist.

As suddenly as he'd pushed me under, he brought me back up. My chest heaved as I attempted to pull in enough air through just my nostrils, my own panties stopping me from gulping mouthfuls.

Once again he shoved me back into the water, once again causing me to grapple with him, once again sending my brain into shock at the lack of oxygen.

This time when he pulled me out, he spun me round and pressed my face into the rock. I shook my head under his hand, kicking back at him when he shoved my dress over my backside and tore at my panties. My hands clawed at his to let me go but his grip only tightened.

He laughed manically. "I'll keep these ones for myself, just in case you run out after sharing your dirty cunt with my staff."

I whimpered, biting onto my panties when he shoved his cock inside me, a sharp hiss coming from him with the dryness that met him. I was struggling to breathe. The way he squashed my face against the rock closed one of my nostrils, my only available input through one side, my mouth stuffed full with my underwear.

"This—is—mine," he grunted with each thrust. "You fucking whore! And just because my baby isn't inside you yet, doesn't mean it won't be, it just means I get to play rough after all."

I was angry at myself when my sobbing blocked my nose with mucus. Bucking under him, trying to tell him I was suffocating, he grunted harder, probably thinking I was aroused and fucking him back. Crazy sadistic bastard! Like what he was doing would turn me on! I couldn't think rationally and I needed my hands to brace myself from the brutal impact his thrusts were having on my face and body.

"You ever touch him or even look at him with those come fuck me eyes, Star," he growled, his pounding frenzied, his hold on my head becoming more and more painful as the rough stone grazed my cheek, "I will kill him! You think I like it rough. Frank's perversion makes mine look docile. We do have one thing in common, though."

He threw pictures down on the rock next to my head.

"He likes to document the breaking of his prize, just like me."

Images of that poor girl, Blue, were on them but I couldn't make them out with my body under so much punishment.

With the thought of violence racing through his mind, he pushed deep inside me and spilled into me, a sharp cry coming from him with his fucked up orgasm.

My chest heaved with what little air I managed to pull through my nose when his hand disappeared with his cock. I daren't move and I remained there, my bare ass stuck up, his semen trickling down my thighs as my face lay against the rock, the salt from my tears stinging my cut skin.

Softly and sickeningly he patted my backside. "Dinner will be ready soon, don't be too long." I gagged when he leaned into me and placed a gentle kiss to the base of my spine, zipped himself up and left.

Waiting until I saw him retreat through the gap between two large pillars, I pulled my panties out of my mouth and vomited all over the rock, my face still laid against it, my own sick seeping under my cheek and into my hair and onto the photos.

A wretched cry left me as I finally slid down and landed in the shallow part of the water, my thighs clenching at the pain between my legs and my chest struggling to accommodate my cries as it still fought to refill my lungs.

I heaved again when the water turned pink, my blood and vomit creating more color in the beautiful but now tainted setting. I grasped up the pictures, dipping them into the water to remove the vomit. My soul cried for her, for me, for the image and memories of a man I thought to be a good man, a protector. How would I ever trust anyone again?

Image after image of torture. Frank grinning at the camera as he was buried inside a broken Blue, bent over what looked like a gymnastic vault. Her torso rested on top, her arms tied on one side, her legs the other, she was completely at the mercy of men who didn't know the meaning of the word. Other pictures showed them using tools of some kind to rape her. How evil these men were left me feeling hopeless.

The secluded area provided privacy for my breakdown as I screamed and cried, wept and wailed, snot and tears and blood mixing in with the water as my despair soiled the serenity.

I cried until the sun went down, and all that left me was whimpers and hiccups, my body using the water I was sat in to cleanse me of the filth Dante had left on and in me.

I took a small gasp when the little bird from earlier landed on the opposite rock, its tiny head tipped to the side as it watched me. Its wide round eyes held onto mine as its sharp beak vibrated, a funny sound coming from it. Suddenly it jumped into the water, dipped its head and brought out another fish. It continued to stare at me, the fish flailing vigorously in its hold, the sound of its flapping as mesmerizing as the bird's gaze.

Slowly, its beak opened as it inclined its head to the water. The fish fell from its mouth, dropped back into the water and swam away. Its beak vibrated again, the tone louder this time before it suddenly took off, soaring above my head, circling once then disappearing over the top of the cliff.

I was going crazy. I must have been. But as my gaze dropped back to the water my eyes caught the movement of the freed fish as it jumped out of the water and dived back in, delighted in its unexplainable freedom.

Taking a big calming breath, I pushed myself up, wincing at the soreness and pulled my wet clothes back down. I swallowed back my tears, pulled my shoulders back and went to join Dante for dinner.

CHAPTER 23

COLD TURKEY

Dante

CLOSING MY EYES, I TRIED to get a grip. My blood was burning, scalding my veins as it raced around my body in search for what it needed.

Fucking Delia. She deserved to die. The bitch had come without the stuff, or she'd ingested it all on her way over because I'd be damned if I could find it in her briefcase. Stupid cunt. I pictured her face when the bullet pierced her tiny fucking brain, the little hole in her head so satisfying. It was the only thing getting me through this damn agony. Well, other than being balls deep inside Star; the sound of her sobbing, the scent of her blood and the sight of her so broken beneath me giving me the most intense orgasm, feeding me the high I needed, even if only for a few minutes.

If I found out she was screwing Frank then they'd both die—painfully. The perverted bastard had done a job on Blue, and Star wouldn't have a clue what hit her when Frank exposed his kink.

A laugh broke free at that thought. Fuck, she thought I was rough!

Malik was up to something too; his fucking knowing stare on me gave me the creeps. The way he watched Star got on my nerves, like he worshipped her. The sad prick, he had no idea how to handle her, or what my little bitch liked. She liked it hard and dirty. But, then so did Malik, his tendency to play with both males and females twisting my gut with disgust. Shit, the ponsy cunt might be after my dick! I shrugged, dismissing that idea immediately. He wouldn't dare! He knew I'd pound him until he resembled shit on a skewer.

My lips were sore, the constant gnawing on them making them raw and split. Fuck, if I didn't get a fix soon I was gonna bust some fucker.

"Finally!" I growled when my call connected and a ringing tone sounded. "Where the fuck you been, Jethro?" I barked as soon as he answered.

He paused, a tight sigh of annoyance echoing down the line. "Mr. Troy, how can I help you today?"

"I need some TSD knocking up, like now."

"Supplies are out," he informed me with a yawn, making my teeth grind together. "Delia emptied the stock yesterday."

"Well get some more fucking stock then!" I snarled. For fuck's sake, did I have to do everything myself? My staff were useless bastards. They were the first to jump to it if their fucking salary didn't credit their bank account every month.

"Mr. Troy, it's not that easy . . ."

"Jethro. You have two options. Either get off your lazy fat ass and sort out fresh supplies, or I'll make sure someone popular takes a two by two and shoves it up your lazy fat ass. Completely your choice."

He went silent, knowing my words weren't said in jest. Fuck, he probably knew it would be me ripping his ass in two with a plank of fucking wood.

"I'll make sure to call you when stocks are replenished."

"Good boy, but don't call me until it's been prepped and is ready to go. Oh, and Jethro, make sure it's today."

"Of course, Mr. Troy."

Asshole.

Fuck, my skin was jumping. This was worse than the usual drug withdrawal. Fucking lying slut had told me it wasn't addictive. I had tweaked the drug and let her add to it over the years to weed out after effects I noticed over time. What was I thinking letting her have a say? Now she was dead and I was vibrating out of my skin. Not addictive, she said, when I told her I felt withdrawal when we became stranded on the island after a bad storm that left us isolated for nearly two weeks. Fuck! I wanted to bring her back so I could go slower with her death. I knew now she'd only told me that so she could get her grubby talons on me. She never thought I'd shoot her.

Lucky for me we had my chemist making up stock for us who then sent it to my outsource guy, Jethro, who distributed to Delia and my clients. So, we had her added recipe and it was just a case of stock.

Another laugh burst from me. Things were finally looking up. Well, they would be as soon as I slipped the little disc into the patch of skin under my arm.

My stomach rumbled when a faint scent of bacon wafted past my nostrils, causing me to frown. When was the last time I'd actually eaten?

A smile lifted my lips. Food would do me good. Well, that and tormenting Star. The way she walked across the room trying not to grab my attention made me chuckle. She didn't realize it was her fear that made my cock throb for her; the terror in her eyes made my blood pump faster. Stupid whore. Cade should have been glad I'd taken her off his hands.

Frank stared at me when I walked into the dining room, laughing at my own internal conversation. Fuck, I frowned *at myself.* I was going crazy. My mind was too active. TSD slowed my brain down, soothing all the rampart parts that refused to shut the fuck up. Hence, my wild ramblings.

Frank quickly turned away when I narrowed my eyes on him. The prick was still under scrutiny. If I caught him with any of Star's underwear again, I'd tear his nuts from his sack and feed them so far up his ass he'd choke on his own fucking pubes.

I shrugged to myself with that thought, half of me hoping I'd find her bra stuffed in his pocket just to see if I could work his cock down his throat like Theo had swallowed the deodorant can.

He eyed me when I chuckled and regarded him. Fucking idiot. They were all fucking idiots. They had no idea they would all be dead within the week anyway. They all needed to go; I couldn't trust any-one and when I made Star my wife and knocked her up I didn't want anyone else there.

"Cheers!" I smirked at him, lifting my glass of juice in the air.

He shrugged then grinned and lifted his own. "Cheers."

Yeah, they were definitely fucking idiots!

CHAPTER 24

HOLDING ON

Faye

"GOOD MORNING." I GREETED DANTE and Frank cheerfully as they sat silently at the dining table. Their gazes slid to me, deep frown lines across their brows.

Trying to hide my smug smile, I walked over to the dresser and poured a glass of juice.

"A good fuck was obviously what you needed." Dante chuckled arrogantly. I could still hear the tight tone in his voice, his withdrawal becoming unbearable. Unfortunately, or rather for the plan I had in my head, fortunately, his temper was constantly simmering just below the surface. "But that's always the case with whores. Dick is a drug, and you always need your fix don't you, Star?"

Ignoring him, I allowed my eyes to soften when they landed on Frank. Taking the chair next to him I smiled at him as I sat beside him. "I'm sorry, about yesterday," I said regretfully. "It was a shock but I'm glad you're here with me." I rested my hand on top of his on the table, giving it a slight squeeze. "I missed you."

I felt the rage bubbling from Dante, and not wanting to push too much too soon, I removed my hand and reached for a croissant, finally giving Dante my attention but making sure to drop the smile. "Is there anything specific you wanted from me today?"

He narrowed his eyes as he stabbed at a piece of his bacon. "Always offering yourself to me, Star. See what I mean about being a whore?"

I smiled and shrugged. He knew exactly what I meant but my nonchalance angered him further. Sliding the bacon off his fork with his teeth, the sound making goose bumps erupt all over me, he smirked. "You're not to leave the house today. I'm not sure right now if I want to fill your dirty cunt or not."

I nodded, holding on to the bile that threatened to choke me. "No problem. I'll be in the studio if you need me."

His eyes narrowed and he tipped his head. "Although I've known for a while that you're mine, Star, I want to know why all of a sudden you've realized that fact."

Frank shifted uncomfortably beside me but I shrugged, pulling at my pastry and popping a small piece in my mouth. "What's the point in fighting you?" I sighed as if I was exhausted and rubbed at my eyes. "I'm not going anywhere, you made sure of that. I need this to be as easy as possible."

Dante pursed his lips and regarded me. "Finally sunk in has it?"

I flicked him a sad glance, forcing tears into my eyes but didn't reply. All he needed to know was that I'd given in, stopped the fight for my benefit and not his.

He sighed loudly and stood. "I'll allow you the morning to paint then I'll come and fetch you. I have plans for us this afternoon."

I swallowed the fear and nodded, noticing the way his fists clenched to stop the shake in his hands. His eyes were bloodshot, the whites tinged with a hint of yellow. What the hell was he on? He was struggling to even breathe.

When he closed the door behind him I turned to Frank. "Could you do me a favor?" He nodded, giving me a soft smile, obviously pleased we were on talking terms. "The studio was set up by Dante for me and everything is haphazard. When I'm painting I like to have things within reach to snatch up quickly before my mind breaks. Can you help me shift the furniture closer to the window please?"

"Sure." He stood up, placing a hand on my shoulder. I forced myself not to recoil, my mind filled with the visions of what he'd done to Blue with those hands. "I'll meet you up there. I have a few things to sort out first."

I smiled widely at him, my eyes flicking to the door when Malik walked through. His gaze was curious when he saw my camaraderie with Frank.

Malik nodded in acknowledgment as Frank passed him, then took Frank's chair beside me and reached for his selection of breakfast. "What's going on?" He didn't look at me but I sensed his suspicion.

"Nothing, I was just asking Frank to help me shift the furniture in the studio."

He blinked. "I'd have helped you, you know that." I frowned at the look of hurt on his face.

"What's going on, Malik?" I asked quietly, hiding our conversation from the cameras.

"Nothing's going on. Just that . . ." He sucked air through his teeth and slid his eyes to mine. "Just be careful with Frank. He's not the man he showed to you. He's cruel and sadistic."

I nodded, placing my croissant back onto my plate as my stomach churned. "I know. I know what he did to Blue."

Malik nodded, lowering his eyes. "He and Hunter both deserve to be fucked in hell for what they did to that girl."

"Hunter?"

"Yeah." He nodded, his jaw clenching with his disgust. "He's what we call a 'Supplier.' He supplies people with whatever they want . . . including motherfuckers who rape and beat women."

I shivered and forced some coffee into my stomach in an attempt to alleviate the nausea.

"Anyway," Malik sighed and rose from his chair. "Just, be careful, yeah?"

I nodded. "I will."

He paused as if he wanted to say something else but turned and left the room instead.

Slumping back in my chair, I took a big breath, fortifying myself from the inside. I wasn't sure I could do this. However, I didn't see another way out. The way Dante was going, if he didn't get a fix soon,

I would die. He wouldn't be able to hold onto his rage forever, and I knew it would only take a single thing to make him snap and take his punishment on me too far.

My heart ached and I closed my eyes picturing Cade's soft smile. "I miss you, baby." Grief forced tears from my eyes but I gulped them back. Tears wouldn't get me anywhere; they'd just drag me down and exhaust me.

And for the next stage, I needed all the energy I could muster.

"HERE?" FRANK ASKED THROUGH CLENCHED teeth as he shifted a large shelving unit across the room. Stalling, I tipped my head back and forth, relishing in his discomfort.

"Hmm. I'm not sure now. No, put it back where it was." Rolling his eyes, he grumbled something and struggled back across the room.

Dante caught my attention through the window when he emerged from the outbuilding, his fingers in his mouth as he chewed on his nails. Looking at the clock, I realized it was already lunch time, so checking Dante was on his way towards the house, I closed my eyes for a moment, building my resolve then gritted my teeth and made my way over to the shelf that housed all the paint pots, dragging a chair with me.

"Frank!" I shouted with a gasp as I gripped the edge of the shelf. "Shit, quick, help me."

I held onto the three paint cans with one hand, my fingers spread precariously as I tried to support them, and pulled on the shelf with my other hand, my legs wobbling as I stretched up on my tiptoes to reach.

"What the hell are you doing?" Frank cried as he shot across the room to help me.

As soon as he reached me, his hand reaching up to mine to hold the shelf, I let go with both hands. The shelf, complete with all three opened paint cans crashed to the floor, splattering both Frank and me in a rainbow of color.

Frank gasped at the same time as me when the chair tipped up and we both went to the floor. He landed on top of me, red paint dribbling down his forehead, his face a palette of various color as red, blue and green acrylic paint oozed down from his hair.

I knew I looked the same. I opened my eyes, staring up at Frank when he did the same and his eyes poked through the goo.

I didn't need to fake my laughter; he looked downright hilarious. He obviously thought the same when he saw me, his lips twitching under the paint before a bark of laughter tore from him.

I joined him, both of us hysterical, both of our bodies writhing on the floor, Frank's huge body only supported by one of his hands as he tried to hold himself above me.

"WHAT THE FUCK?" Dante bellowed.

Both Frank and I froze, our eyes snapping to each other, both of us aware that shit was about to hit the fan.

He scrambled off me, attempting to wipe the paint from his face with hands that were just as covered. "Shelf came down," he said.

Dante was furious, his whole face red with rage, his blazing eyes narrow and flicking wildly from me to Frank then back to me.

"I'm sure it did," he growled taking a step towards us both. "What the fuck are you doing in here?"

Frank frowned, one side of his face scrunching in astonishment at Dante's uncalled fury. "Helping Faye move furniture."

Dante shot his eyes to mine. "Why are you moving things?"

I allowed my gaze to remain on Frank for a couple of seconds before I slid my eyes to Dante. "It's not practical the way it's set up at the moment, that's all."

He regarded me questioningly, his eyes glaring as he tried to read if I was lying. A shiver wracked his body and he winced, bringing his hands to his arms to rub his goose pimpled flesh.

Malik appeared in the doorway, his eyes flicking between us, silent and waiting for Dante to blow off. He held my gaze for a moment, his scrutiny moving from me to Frank, his eyes widening slightly before they went back to Dante.

"Jethro called. He said the stock just came in."

Dante blinked, excitement lighting his face as his attention instantly shifted from Frank and me to Malik. "Already?"

Malik just shrugged, his face stone cold.

Dante turned to me. "I have business to attend to." I lifted a brow. He meant his drugs had been delivered and he needed to go score. However, holding back my smile, I nodded, excitement racing through me with the opportunity I needed falling straight into my lap like a gift from Father Christmas.

"Sure."

I was stunned. His drugs were obviously more important than me if he was willing to leave me alone. My happiness was short lived when he added, "Frank will remain here with you."!

I saw Malik shift uncomfortably and it wasn't until I noticed his unease that my nerves kicked into gear. If Frank had done what he did to Blue, what was he actually capable of?

"I'll stay too," Malik offered.

Dante spun round, query and suspicion in his eyes. Malik leaned into Dante's ear and whispered something. Dante's eyes flicked to Frank before he nodded sternly, thankfully agreeing with Malik and whatever he had advised.

I stiffened when Dante moved quickly across the room to me. Wincing when he snatched my face in his fingers, I tensed, preparing myself for his hatred. He leaned forward, bringing his face into mine as a cruel smirk curled his lip. "I trust you will behave, Star. You know the consequences if you don't!"

Dropping me suddenly, he spun round to Frank. "And don't think I'm not watching you."

Frank sighed, shaking his head, but Dante didn't seem to notice before he turned to Malik. "Watch them both!" Malik gave him a stern nod with the order. Dante flicked Frank and me one last glance, disappearing quickly through the door. "And get cleaned up!"

Frank followed him out, leaving me and Malik silently staring at each other. Finally, he shook his head and sighed. "What are you playing at, Faye?"

"Nothing."

He tipped his head to the side, scowling at me. "I'm not stupid, and neither is Frank. You play him and he won't hesitate to finish what you're starting!"

Pulling my shoulders back, I glared at him, "There is nothing going on, Malik. What the fuck do you care anyway? You're as bad as Dante, so don't start playing games with me because I'm not stupid either! Someone put my panties in Frank's room, and it wasn't me!"

He tensed and turned away, halting at the door. "Dante won't hesitate to kill Frank if he thinks he has a thing for you. But," he continued quietly, "he will be as swift to kill you if he thinks you're fucking Frank behind his back."

I swallowed, knowing he was right, but I didn't see any other way out of this shit. It was all the way or not at all.

"So," he turned to me, locking my gaze in his. "Let me see to this and you just sit back, watch and stay safe."

"Why?" I asked, causing him to pause before he closed the door, his expression one of puzzlement. "Why are you helping me?"

His face tightened and he lowered his eyes, but all he gave me was a shrug before he left me alone.

I couldn't understand why Malik was helping me. He'd been as bad as Dante in the beginning, his cruel taunts just as hurtful.

Sighing, I pushed Malik out of my mind and walked over to the window, my gaze settling on the outbuilding.

All I needed was a diversion and I prayed one came quickly before Dante returned high and horny.

CHAPTER 25

ANSWERED PRAYERS

Faye

IT JUST SO HAPPENED THAT the diversion came in the shape of a football game. A large one, apparently. I had no idea who was playing, hell I had no clue as to what football was about, but when I heard Malik and Frank screaming at the TV, each of them apparently cheering on opposite teams, I knew I would love football for the rest of my damn life.

My heart pounded in my ears as I slid past the media room, their loud shouts giving me the courage to make a run for it, quietly slipping through the kitchen and out through the back door.

I blew out frequent breaths, urging myself to calm the down as I ran through the grounds, trying to keep to the edge and away from the floodlights lighting the estate. I'd never manage it if I passed out before I even got there.

"Shit!" I hissed when a sensor caught me and a light drenched the area in front of Dante's office building.

Closing my eyes and willing my hands to stop shaking, I punched my date of birth into the keypad, grinning when the door clicked.

Bloody fool, he should have changed it after he'd revealed the code to me. I slipped my phone and the USB from my back pocket. The bastard had been so cock sure about me coming back that he'd never even checked my case, although I'd hidden the little gadget in the lining just in case.

"It's me," I whispered quietly. "I'm in."

"You okay?" Kenny asked before I'd even finished my sentence.

"Yeah, did you give Cade my message?" My heart clenched with the thought of him.

"I did. Word for word, babe."

"Thank you."

We both took a silent few moments, Kenny allowing me to build up the courage to do this and me using the moment to appreciate a quick memory of the man I loved.

Shaking myself off, I sighed and nodded my head with determination. "Okay, let's do this."

"Right." He also took a deep breath. "Is there a PC or a laptop? Anything that connects straight to the mainframe?"

"There's all sorts here." I looked around, well out of my depth. I zeroed in on a laptop.

"A laptop on his desk," I answered relieved to see something I actually knew how to use.

"That'll do. Fire it up."

Opening the lid, I groaned when I was met with a password screen. "Shit, it's saying it needs a password!"

"Don't worry. Plug the USB in, Faye."

I slotted the USB into the port. "Right, the cable I gave you. Connect one end to your phone and the other to the USB." He paused, waiting for me to follow his order. As soon as I'd done it, the screen fired to life, row after row of numbers and strange letters scrolling at lightning speed. I started to become disheartened after 'Access denied' flashed up time after time.

"It's okay, just wait," Kenny said. Almost as soon as he'd said it, 'Access Granted' popped up and a new screen emerged, another weird encrypted page of coding rolling up.

"Right, I can take it from here," Kenny said around the noise of keys clicking rapidly.

"You can delete everything?" I asked.

"Faye, babe. Don't worry. This software will find anything with your name attached, then it will link with any other keyword attached to your name. It will be as though you never existed." He chuckled, and I shouldn't have, but I smiled at the contagious sound.

"Okay." Just as I was about to disconnect, I called out his name.

"I'm here," he murmured around furious clinking.

"Thank you. And Kenny, please take care. Dante's losing it. He's already killed his doctor. He's crazy."

"You're telling me to be careful?" He laughed. "You're one tough chick. I can see why Cade's so in love with you."

My heart warmed, an involuntary grin making my chest stutter.

"Hurry," he whispered. "I've already fried the cameras but I'm not sure how long before they notice the connection is severed."

"It's okay, I have the perfect distraction."

He paused, the click of the keys breaking for a moment. "Faye, be careful. Please."

I swallowed back the nerves, my skin prickling with worry. There was no other way out. No other way. I would either die under Dante's hands or die trying to make things right. I had to try. There was no other option. I wouldn't lie down and die, not when there was the faintest chance I could finish this.

I SHIVERED, MAKING MY WAY quickly down the cold corridors, my nerves frayed as my heart stampeded in my chest.

Pushing the door open, squinting at what I might find, a choked sound rushed up my throat when Alex looked at me through small red slits, his eyes sore with the light streaming into the room from the hall.

"Alex!"

I rushed over to him, twisting the lid off the bottle of water I'd brought for him. "Oh my God." He was a mess, his skin camouflaged in blood and dirt, horrid blue and purple bruises covering his face.

He gulped at the water as I held it to his mouth and tipped, his greed causing him to cough and splutter, the water dribbling down his chin.

"Slowly," I urged, angling the bottle lower so he only received small trickles. "Listen, I'm sorry but I can't get you out yet." He blinked at me, the disappointment heavy with his sigh. "But I'm coming back soon."

"Don't . . ." he rasped, licking at his chapped lips to moisten them with his wet tongue.

"It's okay." I nodded, confirming my words. "There's something I have to do first but then I'll be back."

He eyed me warily but nodded slowly. "Just be careful."

"I will," I promised as I stroked some blood clogged strands of hair off his face, knowing they must have been annoying him. What a dark, vulgar world Dante became a part of. How many people had been kept down here for torture or sick games? I couldn't think about that.

He squeezed his eyes closed and nodded.

This was my fault. I should have known Dante would be watching, and as it turned out, listening to everything I did. I had put Alex where he was, and it was up to me to get him out.

Racing back up, I grabbed my phone. Kenny had finished with what he needed to do, and I ran back through the gardens and up to the house. Coming to a stop just before going back in, my phone rang. Bracing myself and smiling at how things were going exactly to plan, I answered immediately, making sure to put on a terrified voice.

"Star?" His voice was high-pitched. He'd obviously not scored yet. I'd been banking on that too and for a change, things were going in my favor.

"Dante!"

He paused, hearing my fear. "Star, are you okay? The feed to the cameras has been severed? What's going on there? I can't get hold of Frank or Malik." Thank God. Kenny was amazing. He'd followed through with his assurance that he could block Frank and Malik's signal and I owed him a nice long holiday somewhere hot and tranquil.

"Dante. Please come home. Frank . . . he's. . . ."

"He's what?" I remained silent, dramatically panting down the phone. "He's what, Star?"

"He's . . . oh God, when you found my panties, that's not all." I let out a tight whimper. "I think he's developed an unhealthy attraction to me. I've just caught him taking photos of me, Dante, while I was getting undressed."

"What?" He was quiet, almost calm. Too calm. I shivered at the ice in that single word.

"Well," I let out a choked sob. "I've felt someone watching me for the last couple of days. Nothing specific, just a feeling. I thought it was Malik. Fuck, Dante, I thought it was Malik!"

"Where are you?"

"I'm in my room. He's scaring me, Dante. I don't know what to do!"

"Stay there. Do—not—move until I get there. I'm already on my way back."

He cut the call, leaving me on the porch steps with a continuous beep resounding in my ear. The tone matched the beat of my heart, the hurried rhythm in line with the pounding of my pulse.

This was it. Do or die. And I was determined not to die. I needed to keep my heart beating for Cade.

Things were going to plan and I took it as an omen. So giving myself a fortifying nod, I opened the door and stepped inside.

CHAPTER 26

SACRIFICES

Faye

MY HEART PUMPED ADRENALINE AROUND my body, giving me the courage I needed. Timing was crucial. Dante was nearly home and the game had ended twenty minutes ago. I wasn't sure where Malik was but I knew Frank had gone for a shower and this was the only chance I would get.

I tiptoed through the house until I came to the door leading me to the room Frank was staying in. Taking a few gulps of air to try and steady myself, I pushed the door ajar and slipped in. The scent of man sweat was pungent in the air, my nose wrinkling as a sweet smell assaulted me as well. What was it about men and smells? He needed to open a window.

I scanned the room briefly before creeping over to the bedside table and opening it, pulling the pictures which were once a fond memory of Cade capturing me in my most natural state, changing, sleeping. He wanted what no one else got to see . . . the real me, and now I was using them in a fucked game Dante had forced me to play. I needed the upper hand to turn them on each other. I pulled the last one from my bra and dropped it with the others inside. I felt so dirty, my whole body shivering with the disgust of what I was about to do. But I needed to do it. I had to.

Lifting my dress, I slipped my panties down my thighs and kicked them towards the base of his bed, just enough so they could be seen.

The shower turned off and I blew out a breath, trying to still my frayed nerves. This was it. It was too late to change my mind, not that I would anyway. I'd had enough. I needed to do this for Cade. And for Jenson and Blue. Their lives would never be the same again and my heart ached for them.

I tore open the top of my dress, the buttons flying in all directions, a small ping echoing in the silence when one hit the mirror and bounced off.

I held my breath, sinking my teeth into my bottom lip so I didn't cry out as I braced my whole body. From my knees to the junction of my thighs I dug my nails in and tore upwards. I saw some of the wounds on Blue; this bastard liked to claw at his victims, a predator marking his prey, playing with it before devouring it. I knew I could take one hit if he didn't use his full strength, and hopefully that was all it would be before Dante came in and found the scene.

My senses were hyper alert, everything sounding and feeling so much more intense. A click of the bathroom door unlocking—*Thud!* The handle dropping—*Thud!* The door swinging open—*Thud!* My heart panicking—*Thud, Thud!*

"What the fuck happened to you?" He was still wet, water beading over his powerful frame. Fuck, he was huge. Maybe I wouldn't be able to take a hit. I slowly took a step back, the extra distance, albeit it tiny, giving me that little bit more courage before I answered.

"Dante happened."

His brow furrowed as he looked to the door then back to me. "He's back? He did that to you?"

I laugh mechanically, shaking my head and telling him no. Shit, I felt crazy, my frantic heartbeat making me dizzy. "You did this to me."

He tightened the towel around his waist, his eyes narrowing in confusion. "What the hell, Faye?"

"Don't you mean Star? Dante's Star?" Taking another step back, I drew in a breath and went for it. "PLEASE DON'T!" I called out, flinching from the change in Frank's demeanor, but sheer determination allowed me to do what was needed. "NO!" I screamed again. "DON'T. PLEASE DON'T!"

His body stiffened, his lip curling up into a sneer. "You ungrateful little cunt. I took care of you, killed for you and this is how you repay me?" His slow menacing steps towards me had me backing up quickly against a wall. "I thought that spineless prick Malik was planting shit. Nearly strangled him with his own cock last night." His palm swiped out down my cheek. "You want your fucked up boyfriend to believe what, Faye? What is this? An affair? An assault?"

I gritted my teeth. "You'd know all about assault Frank!"

His head tilted to the side, his intense blue eyes studying me before a sadistic grin spread across his lips. "Ahh, that's what he wanted the pictures for. Did he show you all the nasty things I did, Faye? Try to frighten you, because it clearly hasn't worked. Here you are practically naked, begging for me to hurt you."

"Fuck you, you animal." I spat in his face.

"I've never let you see that side of me but you came looking for it and if you want to play games, Faye, let's make them look realistic." His hand slipped from my cheek to grip my throat, his arm rising up with me attached. My feet tried to keep the ground beneath them but he was a lot stronger than I anticipated. Where the fuck was Dante? He should have been back by now.

My hands gripped his wrist as I choked for breath.

Bringing my face towards his, he kissed the tip of my nose. "Bye, sweetheart." He palmed my ass with his free hand, raising me higher before throwing me across the room. I lost my breath when my body impacted with the top of a dresser, the ornaments smashing under my weight and some clattering to the floor. My ribs screamed, and before I could do anything, a hand gripped my hair, pushing me down.

"That is a cute ass." His other palm came down hard to smack my ass cheek. "You have no panties on. Is that an invitation? I've never really seen you that way but it would make your scene more believable, right?"

Fuck! No, no, no. I shot my eyes to the door, the first time in my life praying for Dante to walk through it. This wasn't how it was supposed to play out. Why the hell did nothing ever go right?

He wrenched my head back, whispering in my ear. "I'll pretend you're that whimpering little cum bucket, Blue."

I reared my arm back as hard as I could, ramming my elbow into his ribcage.

He released me with a shove. A sinister belly laugh ripped from him, the sound making me shiver. "Nice effort. I like my toys to be riled up before I fuck every hole they have."

I would rather die than let another man touch me that way again. "You're an animal!"

He smirked. "I may be, sweetheart, but she was a slut and everyone knew it. She liked being used up. Her body was built for a big bad cock like mine. She's a snake, leading Jenson, the stupid fuck, on all that time and fucking everything else with an erection."

I swiped at some blood I felt trickling down my lip. My tooth must have pierced my lip when I hit the dresser. "So, she deserved what you did to her?" I asked, incredulous.

"She broke rules, Faye, betrayed what she was paid to do and could have got Dante killed. Betrayal has consequences and Dante gave me the pleasures of dishing them out. You know better than anyone that retribution is something Dante takes seriously." He chuckled.

"Oh, I do know. And he's going to want it on you when he knows what you did." I smirked.

"You mean what I'm about to do." He took a step towards me with each word he spoke. "I'm going to fuck your ass, tear you up nice and good. Fuck, I might even taste the blood that pours from you, savor you on my tongue before I kill you and dump you in Malik's room."

My mouth dropped open in shock and fear. "You don't have time," I rushed out.

"Then I'll have to be quick." The back of his hand came out fast, so fast I didn't have time to move before it cracked me across the cheek. Pain exploded, making my eyes water and buckling my knees.

His meaty palm wrapped around my ankle. I kicked out, catching him off guard, causing him to stumble backwards straight into a full length mirror that stood in the corner of the room. The shards rained down behind him and I took the opportunity, pushing up to my knees and crawling away.

His foot hit my backside with power, sending me face first into the floor. My nose popped, a deep cry bursting from me with the pain as a warm river flowed from it. Motherfucker.

"You keep flashing that gash at me Faye . . ." His fingers gripped me by the back of the neck, lifting me clean off the floor and pushing me forwards onto the bed. "And I will fuck it."

With every ounce of hate, fear and strength I had left, I thrashed and screamed and kicked and attacked, scratching and slapping at him, gouging at his skin with my nails as I tried to bite at his flesh.

He mocked me with a laugh. I was no match for him. I should have known Dante would be late; he always ruined everything. It was funny, really. I'd always thought it would be Dante that took my last breath from me, but a man who had been my friend, a father figure for many years, was going to rape me and watch in delight as he snuffed my existence out easily and with as much pain as he could deliver.

Thump.

My eyes bulged and relief burst from me when I saw Malik instead of Frank. He dropped a lamp he must have picked up to hit Frank with.

I sat forward and looked down at Frank who was out cold on the floor.

My mouth fell open as a scream tore from me, shock and relief all coming out of me in a high pitched wail.

CHAPTER 27

SEEING RED

Dante

I WAS ANXIOUS TO GET home and hide away while I medicated. Star mentioned feeling uneasy on the phone about Frank. She caught him taking pictures of her and she was growing worried about the new development of his *unhealthy attention.* God, she always prettying up situations with words. He was fucking perving on her; he and Malik probably planned Delia coming here without my drugs so I'd have to leave and they could be there with Star. Fuck! My mind was driving me crazy.

I didn't give the boat a chance to fully stop before I was off it and bounding up the dock.

Opening the front door, Star's screams greeted me and turned my body to stone. My heart forgot to beat as my head screamed numerous scenarios at me, my body on auto-pilot as I ran through the house towards her screams.

Nothing prepared me when I burst into the room. Star was in complete disarray, her body beaten, her dress in tatters, and her mouth wide open, screams ripping from her one after the other as Malik stood over her.

Red was all I saw. It blanked out every rational or human thought in my head. It demanded to be fed. It demanded liberation.

In a haze of movements, almost like I had stepped out of my body and was watching the scene unfold from a distance, I moved into the room, bent to pick up a shard of broken mirror, then leapt across the bed and jammed it straight into Malik's neck. His hot blood sprayed over my face, making me blink with each spurt that slapped my skin. His eyes enlarged, pure disbelief and shock in them as his mouth dropped open to make a gargling noise. *Yeah you're dying mother-fucker, believe it.*

I pulled the mirror free and then stabbed him in the groin, over and over in a fit of unkempt rage; euphoria and ecstasy flowed through every single blood vessel in my body. "I FUCKING WARNED YOU!" I screamed, deafening out Star's hysteria.

His body had fallen into me. I shrugged him off and shivered, looking down at my shaking hand, my blood and his mingling together; he got to share fluids with me after all.

I dropped the glass and winced from the raw wound on my palm, and that was when I noticed an unconscious Frank in nothing but a towel, Malik's dead eyes staring up at me from next to him, blood draining from him in a current of dark crimson pools.

Fuck. I'd known him a long fucking time and I'd butchered him.

"It was Frank! It was Frank! It was Frank!" Her erratic screams repeated.

What? It was Frank?

"Don't fucking move." My eyes turned to the door to see Jenson holding a gun at me! And I'd left mine in my study because my mind wasn't functioning right.

Oh, great! And in came my asshole brother. I should have killed him when I had the chance—In the womb with the cord wrapped around his neck.

Fuck!

I reached down, grabbed the shard and dragged Star against my chest, holding the piece of mirror to her throat. I would never kill her but they didn't need to know that. "Stay away, fucker, or I'll pop her artery!"

Her body jerked so much from her sobs that my bloody hands kept slipping off her.

"Calm down, baby, it's okay," I soothed in her ear.

A loud snap rang out. My body jolted as my right shoulder set on fire, an agonizing pain bursting through me. What the fuck?

I fell backwards off the bed with Star in my arms, our bodies landing with a heavy thud on the floor. I felt it; the mirror cut into her. I had never felt sick from the violence I inflicted but the uncertainty of what I just did because that punked up little prick shot me made my insides spin, and chaos ran rampant in my head. She fell from me, her body rolling on to Frank and Malik.

CHAPTER 28

SO MUCH BLOOD

Cade

EVERYTHING HAPPENED SO FAST; THE gun shot fire rang out and the grunt from Dante, and then they fell. What the fuck had he been doing to her? She looked like she had been messed up pretty bad and was in shock. We waited too long to come get her.

Jenson raced around the bed to keep his gun on Dante but something stilled his attention. Everything was in slow motion as I prepared myself for seeing if my girl was okay.

I couldn't hear her. I couldn't hear anything but the slow thud in my chest.

I rounded the bed and swallowed down the cry of relief. Faye was leaning over someone else, her hands covered in blood, holding the man's neck. He was as white as a ghost, his eyes lifeless and staring. It was Malik.

I booted Dante in the face, knocking him out before he could taunt, making either me or Jenson end him early.

"I'm so sorry," my girl sobbed, her face buried in Malik's chest, her palms spread over his face. Frank lay next to them both, blood

153

seeping from a wound on his head.

"Is he dead?" Jenson gestured with his chin to his still form. I reached under Faye's armpits and lifted her from the dead guy then moved away as Liam, Blue's dad, and numerous guys piled in the room and checked his pulse.

"No, he has a pulse."

"Good," Jenson said, going over to stand above him. He lifted his foot and brought it back down hard on Frank's crotch area over and over.

I spun Faye in my arms and covered her face, keeping her from witnessing Jenson's rage.

"Enough!" Liam commanded from the doorway. "Show us where the cells are. I want the names of the other two. One of these will speak when they see what happened to the others for not talking. Someone should wait with the girl."

She pushed from my body, shaking her head. "Don't leave me with someone else, Cade, please. I need to know they're not coming back for me."

"They won't be coming for anyone ever again." I reassured her, swiping across her cheekbone with my thumb and wiping away the river of tears.

"I need to see it. I need to see them die."

Damn, I didn't want her to have to live with seeing that. This wasn't going to be a clean kill. We needed information on this Hunter guy.

"Let the woman have her closure, son," Liam agreed. "She can watch the final trigger kill. Bring her."

"Baby . . ."

"I need to, Cade. I need to put an end to the nightmares. Malik . . ." She squeezed more tears from her eyes, grief and sadness consuming her. "I owe it to Malik. He saved my life and he tried to get me out of here. And now he's dead!"

Her pale face and her bruised and broken body crippled my heart. She didn't deserve this, none of it. She would have nightmares for many years for what Dante had done to her, so what did one more matter if it would help bring her the closure she needed?

I held up my hands in surrender. She nodded. I had a feeling it would be a while before she ever smiled again, and I made a promise to myself that I would make sure she would have plenty to smile about in her future.

Taking her hand in mine, I gave it a squeeze. "You need to show us where Alex is."

She sighed and looked up at me. "He's a mess, Cade. I managed to get some water down him earlier."

"Don't worry, he'll be okay. I promise." She couldn't cope with any more deaths on her conscience. "Baby, none of this is your fault. This is my brother's twisted mess, not yours."

She swallowed but didn't answer me. "We need to hurry," she urged as she pulled me to the door and led us into what would soon become hell.

I WAS GLAD FAYE HAD decided to stay outside the room in the end, her need to aide Alex greater than her need to watch Frank become pig fodder.

Shit. Liam and his guys didn't mess about. Turned out Blue kept secrets. She learned her skills for making unbreakable codes and security from a very dangerous daddy. Known in the black market diamond fighting trade as 'Slicer,' he did time in his teens for cracking a safe and getting away with a million in diamonds. When a single police officer on the scene tried to stop him, he beat him with a pen holder from a teller's desk and then sliced into his cheek, taking a small sliver of flesh as a souvenir. He was picked up three days later at another bank and served a ten year sentence. When he was released he merged into the underworld and quickly built himself a scary repetition. I only heard of his name at the underground fights because people there used to work for him and when you do anything a little illegal, the Chinese whispers circulate about the biggest players. I wanted no part of that world anymore, or him, but this wasn't just my revenge now. We shared it. They'd annihilated Frank; tortured him so much that my stomach wouldn't be able to hold anything for a fair few months.

Frank's piercing scream bounced off the walls as Liam slid the fillet knife down his chest, peeling his skin away from the dense pectoral muscle, the slice so thin that the skin curled like apple peel and dropped onto Frank's foot. "I can keep this up all night, motherfucker." Liam sighed contentedly, relishing in Frank's pain as he twirled the tip of the knife around Frank's right nipple, tormenting him.

Stupidly, Frank remained silent and I cringed when Liam dug out his nipple easily. As a child I'd watched my mother prepare potatoes with a small knife. She would peel the skin and then dig out the eyes with the tip. Watching Liam work, I wondered if he had also helped his mother prepare vegetables in his childhood.

When he dragged the knife up the center of Frank's chest and up the center of his throat, piercing the skin enough to leave a trickle of blood behind, and then brought it up to Frank's eye, I prayed that Frank started to wise the hell up because I wasn't savoring the thought of watching him have his eyelid removed.

"Fine!" he spluttered, his surrender generating a heavy sigh of relief from me. "I don't know his address but I have his number. That's all I can give you!"

Liam turned to Jenson, tilting his head in question. I gave Liam his due, he'd made sure to include Jenson in the whole thing. Jenson nodded, giving his approval. "It's all we have but it's a start."

"It'll do," I butted in, an idea forming in my head.

Liam nodded, jotting down a phone number as Frank relayed it from memory, making we aware that Hunter was good at covering his back, no information stored other than in people's heads. He then slid his firearm from the back of his jeans and held it out to Jenson. "Straight shot to the pelvis," he instructed, causing Frank's eyes to widen. "It's the most painful. Make this fucker pay before you force his last breath from him."

"You bastard!" Frank hissed out, "I gave you Hunter's number. Make it clean. Even in our world there's ethics!"

Liam laughed loudly, his face contorting into something quite disturbing. "Ethics?" He barked out suddenly, aiming the gun at Frank's kneecap and firing quickly. "Where were your ethics when you ripped my daughter to fucking pieces like an animal?"

Frank screamed again when Liam took out his other kneecap, the piercing sound making my ears hum as Frank sagged in the cuffs holding him up. Tears streamed down his face but all I could picture was the photos of Blue, her blood-stained, pale face smeared in her tears. I was glad this fucker got to pay with his own.

Jenson took the gun from Liam but I pulled him to one side before he could take a shot. He stared at me curiously. "Jen." I swallowed, closing my eyes for a second. "You need to think about what this means." He shook his head in confusion. Biting my lip, hating the heaviness that never left my chest, I lowered my voice. "You take his life then that's it for the rest of yours. I know how much this means to you, your hunger for vengeance. But once you're a killer, you're forever a killer."

"Cade?" His gaze was soft, worried as he lay a hand on my shoulder.

"I . . . you know when I fought in the scene. I was a mess. I had watched my brother bring down the girl I loved every day, watched him grind her soul into despair with every snide remark to her, every time he was disrespectful, every time I watched her curl into a corner and cry because she didn't know how to handle his dark side and she loved him anyway and was hurting that he was leaving. But he was my brother, Jen." He nodded, giving me his understanding. "So the fights, they helped me get it out. The day I witnessed Faye have the abortion to give Dante a chance at his collage and career, fuck man, I . . . it fucked me up. Why should she pay so dearly because of what he wanted? She was a mess, she hated herself. I took her home the following day and I was so strung out, I went to fight. You remember?"

Jenson studied me, his eyes locked onto mine as he nodded.

"I fucked him up bad, Jen. All I could see was Faye's distress and Dante's fucking face, laughing and mocking." I paused, swallowing back the bile. "I didn't stop hitting him, even when I knew he'd had enough. Eddie was our friend and I hit him one time too many and took his life! That marked me. You think it soothes the rage and brings you a new prospective but instead it creates a new rage bubbling under the surface."

"Shit, man," Jenson sighed, squeezing my shoulder.

157

"You won't ever let it go, Jenson. It will go with you everywhere. Frank's death will be part of your life forever. I need you to understand that."

He blew out a breath but nodded. "I know, but for Blue, I'd carry the damn devil on my back for eternity. She's my woman. Fuck, I love her. I know she doesn't love me, but you know what, I don't care right now. I can't sleep knowing what they did to her. I can't breathe without picturing her, in pain, un . . . under them." His eyes filled up and my heart broke for him. "They fucking wrecked her, Cade. They tore her up so bad she'll never have kids." His hand slapped over his mouth as he retched. "No way. No fucking way will they take another breath. And I want to take their last from them. Do you understand that?"

I nodded, giving him a knowing smile. "More than you think."

His eyes flicked to Dante and he nodded back at me. "It's time to man up. Prove to her what she means to me." I think she already knew but I let him go with it. I just couldn't let him do this without warning him how much it would alter his life. But at the end of the day, it was Jenson's life, not mine, and I understood completely why he needed to do this.

He walked back across the room and before he could change his mind, took aim and fired a hole though Frank's pelvis. His scream was silent this time, his head lulling backwards as his body began to give in.

"Not yet, cunt!" Jenson spat as he shoved the gun inside Frank's mouth and angled it upwards. "I hope you burn in hell!"

I watched as Frank's brain fired out the back of his head and splattered the wall, bits of skull and flesh spraying the grey concrete floor in a dramatic splash of color.

I turned, my heart stilling when I witnessed Faye in the open door, her eyes trained on Frank as a tear rolled down her face.

"Hey," I breathed, rushing over to her and pulling her face to my chest.

"I loved him, Cade," she whispered, the tight sound of her grief making my eyes water. "I loved him like a father. How could he?"

Sighing, I pulled her further against me. "Only God knows where greed will take us, Faye."

"Hell," she whispered in return. "Greed takes us to hell."

"And may he fucking burn there," Jenson finished quietly.

I COULDN'T HELP BUT GRIN at Dante as he swung where Frank had hung, his bare feet scraping through Frank's brain matter that still decorated the floor. The gag around his mouth made me happy, so did the bruising to his face and torso. It was surreal gaining pleasure from seeing my replica hurting. I loved him once but this cruel, ruthless man was not the kid I shared everything with as a child. He had destroyed that person with the crap he kept injecting into his body over the years. He was never truly all there but just how far gone he was made me not see the boy he once was. All I could see was a man who tortured the woman I love. The man who shot me. Kidnapped Blue and Alex and terrorized them. I saw a man I couldn't possible let live. He didn't deserve to live.

"Hunter, it's Dante," I spoke when the call connected.

"Hey, what's up?" Hunter greeted as Dante thrashed in his restraints, his eyes narrow and blazing at me.

"I'm having a little . . .," 'Dinner *party,*' Faye mouthed. "Dinner party," I said down the line to Hunter. "The guys who . . . shall we say *partied* with Blue, I need you to bring them with you. Star's in need of a little lesson."

"What? You bored with her already?"

"She's driving me nuts with all her fucking whining. Stupid whore disrespects me, does the complete fucking opposite to what I tell her. Fuck, she's even stopped fighting with me when I fuck her. She needs to understand what happens if she plays with fire. You have any bitches to bring with you that will entertain what I need?"

"Of course, but are you sure? You saw what they did to Blue, they won't hold back with Star either."

I laughed and clicked my tongue. "Why do you think I need the bitches? Watching that scene play out, fuck, I'm gonna need a slut who takes it hard."

Hunter chuckled. "Then it will be a pleasure." I gritted my teeth to his obvious delight at the thought of causing Faye pain. Motherfucking bastard. I clenched my fist, reining it in.

"Oh," I added quickly. "Bring some brown with you. I need a high."

He paused for a moment then said, "Sure."

Ending the call I tapped Dante on the cheek and winked. "Time to play."

CHAPTER 29

BLOOD IS THICKER THAN WATER

Dante

I SMIRKED WHEN THE TWO guys were dragged into the room by Liam's men.

Chuckling, I opened the only eye they hadn't ruptured and grinned at Cade. "You fucking fool. As soon as you told Hunter to bring some brown he knew it wasn't me. I don't touch that shit, Cade. I only consume what I make; it's the only thing I trust."

Cade shrugged. "Don't worry, Hunter will get his. I'm fascinated by how easily he gave up his two men though."

I laughed. "You really are stupid. He hasn't paid them yet." Hunter was the lowest bastard out there. He had no scruples. And Cade had given him an opportunity to save him thousands.

I flicked my eyes to the scene playing out at the other side of the room. Jenson stood by the door, watching the brutal gang rape of the two men who had hurt his girl so much she wouldn't walk for a long time.

I shivered, looking away when one of them drew a long iron baton and shoved it so far up the blond's ass that I wouldn't have been surprised if it emerged out of his mouth. Their screams were loud and ugly, blood splashing everywhere as I tried to hold onto my stomach.

Unable to watch when they started hacking at their dicks I turned my back on them and prayed my death would be swift and clean.

Eventually the room quietened, the silence confirming their brutal death.

Jenson walked over to Cade, his pale face telling me he had made himself watch every second in respect for Blue, his hand delivering the final blow.

"We'll be outside."

Cade nodded, giving him a faint smile as he patted his shoulder. Then he turned to me, his face full of sadness.

"This is it then." I eyed him just as sadly.

Cade sighed, his eyes lifting to mine. "What the fuck happened to you?" He wasn't angry, just resigned.

"Love." I answered simply. "But in that one little word are so many others we forget about, brother." He blinked at me, his face tight with emotion. "Jealousy. Control and greed. Desperation and insecurity. And we mustn't ever forget possessiveness." He dropped his eyes, closing them for a second. "And they're only some of them, Cade. I loved Star with everything I had. I breathed for her, lived for her. Yet somewhere deep inside, both our insecurities drowned the good parts, the parts that love should be about."

He shook his head. "They only control if you let them, Dante. You were strong, so strong. I idolized you, you're my big brother. Only by a couple of minutes, but we came as a unit. I never saw the moment one of us destroyed that."

"The moment we both fell in love with the same woman, Cade."

He nodded, verifying the truth of my words.

"I loved you both but she was mine, I needed her," I whispered, the pain of finality making my heart still. "Promise . . ." I blew out a breath and smiled sadly. "Promise you'll love her like she deserves."

He snapped his teeth together, sucking in a deep breath before he turned away, gathering the strength he needed.

"And I loved you," he whispered as he pressed the muzzle of the gun to my forehead gently.

I watched as a single tear rolled down his cheek. I nodded to him,

holding his gaze as a tear left my eye, the twin to his. "Do it, Cade."
He knew if he didn't kill me and let me live I would have to kill him.
The fury would come back tenfold to me and demand I take his life.
He didn't have a choice, kill or be killed. "Be happy. Make her happy."

"I promise," he whispered as he pulled the trigger and freed my
soul from the pain of obsession for possession of another soul.

CHAPTER 30

SAD

Cade

I WAS SCARED TO DEATH of finally pulling that trigger. It was like killing a part of myself. I felt it; the pain of killing my own flesh and blood, but with it the cleansing relief of knowing Faye was safe.

She was on the floor outside the doorway when I left the room. Her eyes wrenched open as she battled not to show her sadness. I wouldn't judge her for showing human weakness. He was a bastard but a bastard we loved once.

Scooping her up into my arms we left his place in flames. Destroyed the evidence of us ever being there.

3 DAYS LATER

WE TOLD THE HOSPITAL STAFF Faye took a fall down the stairs. They didn't believe us if the deadly looks I received were anything to go by but they were paid an exceedingly stupid amount for their discretion.

It was the first time I had ever felt uncomfortable in my own house with Faye. She had showered and was standing in a pair of her slouch pants and one of my t-shirts, her face bruised and full of sorrow. I didn't know what to say to her. Was she grieving for him, Malik, Frank? Did she want to be there?

"I can take you home if you want?"

Her head shot up to look at me, a look of panic in her expanding eyes. Her teeth came out to worry her bottom lip and her fingers dug into the side of her thigh, her nervous actions making me wince slightly. "Can I . . . ? Please don't make me go back there alone, Cade."

I walked over to where she was standing, taking her hands away from her damaging her already torn up legs. "I don't want you to go, Faye, I just don't know what you're thinking. For the life of me I can't think what you need from me right now." I hated this. She was everything. I always knew how to read her emotions but she was a new person now, we both were.

Her hands gripped mine. "It's not him." I closed my eyes. She was always aware of what I was thinking. "Dante died a long time ago. I didn't know who that man was, Cade. He was an animal and stole things I can never recover." I implored her with my eyes to keep talking. Her own eyes softened. "He stole us. He made me into someone I despise." She was so defeated. He had broken my girl, dimmed her spark and beat down her spirit. "If you knew, you wouldn't want me here," she stuttered.

Damn, should I tell her I know? If I didn't she would always live in fear that I would one day find out somehow and turn my back on her which was impossible. Dante wasn't the other half of me, she was. She was my other half, she completed the man I was, the man I wanted to be for her. My soul was created with hers and sent here for us to find each other. Love wasn't condemning your soul mate for actions out of their control. Granted, love is painful, the most painful thing we endure on this earth but it's also non-judgmental; it's shameless and freeing the other person of all the things they find imperfect about themselves because to the person that loves them there is no such thing. Love is pure, true, enduring and for me, everlasting. I would love her forever and cherish the time we had. Love like ours was strong, intense and beautiful. Nothing she did without being right of mind could dirty how pure our love was.

"Faye." I lifted my hand, gently cupping her cheek, my heart sighing contently with the simple touch of her. "I know what you went through and that you're punishing yourself for it. It was abuse, baby, no matter what you tell yourself or what he told you."

Her breath shuddered, her tremble coming back with a force. Fuck, would she ever recover from this? "Do you know?" she asked softly.

I knew she was asking me if Kenny showed me and I needed her to know I had seen her at her worst and still loved her with the same passion and ache as I always had. "You said in your message, 'I know that thread is broken now,' but with us it's never broken. It may have frayed for a short time but it can never be broken. I know what he did to you and I know he stole your memory and fed you a lie." Her pale face showed her shame as her eyes lowered but I placed my finger under her chin and tilted her head back until her eyes were where they belonged—on me. "Don't you ever be ashamed of what happened. You were a victim, Faye. Men like Dante have an ability to turn your body against you." I knew that was what was eating away at her and it was almost choking me to think and say it but she enjoyed some of the acts before she knew the truth and it was only natural for her body to react. I wanted to scrub my eyes with bleach and my memory of the images of it all but I couldn't punish her any more than she was punishing herself.

"I'm so ashamed," she choked out, her tiny shudders shaking the foundations of my heart. I wanted to fix her and take it all away but I was out of my depth.

I pulled her fragile body into mine, resting her head against my chest, my chin sitting gently on her head as my arms encompassed her in my shelter. Her tears soaked into my shirt. I just wished I could cleanse her of the consuming pain.

"Can you ever love me again, Cade?"

Oh fuck, I was dying from her pain.

"Do you know what I see and feel when I look at you?" She brought her hands up to wipe the tears covering her face and shook her head, her brows pinching together. "Boundless beauty." I swiped as more tears trickled down her blotchy face. "Astonishing strength." I stroked her hair back. "An enveloping need in my chest to touch you, share your air, your life, your love." I stared into her searching eyes. "I see a divine ecstasy that only you bring me." I placed a soft and fleeting kiss to her lips. "I see my future."

"I'm sorry to intrude." Amy's voice came into the room, breaking us from our moment. Amy moved across the room and launched herself into me and Faye. "You didn't call! You said you would when you had her safe."

Fuck, what a douche. I should have remembered Amy was waiting on news.

"I was going out of my mind!"

Faye flinched and pulled away from us both. "I'm sorry, Amy, my mind was all over the place and Faye needed medical attention."

She turned to survey Faye. "Are you okay?" Her tone dropped to soothing as her eyes roamed every inch of Faye's bruised and broken body.

"Just glad to be home," Faye replied and smiled over at me. I stilled, savoring her goddamned stunning smile. "I need to sleep if that's okay?" she murmured.

"Oh, God, sure. I'm sorry, I was just so worried."

I gripped Amy's shoulder and led her out of the room calling out, "Go lay down, Faye. I'll fix some food and bring it up for when you wake up." I didn't have a clue how to cook but Amy could make herself useful.

"Okay, thank you."

CHAPTER 31

AMY

Faye

BLOOD EVERYWHERE, EACH BRUTAL PLUNDER and squelch of the piece of mirror I had caused to smash pushing into the flesh of a man who was there to save me. He had told me not to play Frank and I ignored him, and got him killed.

Dante was like a possessed demon, showered in the blood of his once good friend. I would never get those images out of my mind.

I brought my hand up to the cut on my neck. I could have died, our blood swirling together. I had made it, though. What Dante had done to all of us affected and changed us forever. Alex may never be able to practice again. Blue may never birth children. Jenson was a killer, and Cade witnessed someone who he once loved die at his own hand.

I couldn't close my eyes without hearing the final gunshot, the sound forever ricocheting around my head. It was over but it wasn't. It lived inside me, haunting me. It was sickening watching the life leave someone. Our scars would heal though, I was with Cade and he still cared about me.

His beautiful words echoed inside my chest, creating a new beat. He knew how to reawaken me. He was always the one I was supposed to love because his love for me was astonishing, intense and unwavering. It was all around me, empowering and soul consuming.

I had given up at low points, imprisoned by Dante's hate. He broke my sprit but Cade knew how to heal me with just words and his embrace. I was heartbroken and Cade knew how to mend my heart with one brief kiss. My mind would take longer; Malik's shocked face as Dante struck stole my breath every time it flooded my thoughts. I couldn't control them, they took my thoughts hostage. I wanted to sleep it all away. Time would heal everything, the doctor said with a pat on the knee. I needed time to pass and for me to be healed of this guilt and regret.

I was clean from a shower but still felt dirty. The sticky, hot blood stained me. I wished this was all a dream. It felt like I had fallen asleep and woken up in a role of one of my characters.

I lay there for an hour and decided I couldn't take the sweet aromas filling the air any longer; my stomach was eating itself.

I made my way towards the delicious smells and voices of Amy and Cade. Music was playing from an iPod and Amy was miming the lyrics to a Beneath Innocence song. They looked so at home together in the kitchen cooking. I couldn't blame him for seeking comfort in her. I had been fucking his brother, I couldn't really condemn him for needing someone, but the pain still stung worse than any other.

The doorbell rang causing both of them to lift their heads from the preparation they were concentrating on. Cade grinned at her and she slapped his shoulder playfully, rolling her eyes. God, I felt like an intruder, looking in at a happy couple playing house. She was so freaking nice too. Always helpful, and so lovely and attentive to me. How could she be that way if she had feelings for him? I wanted to attack her with nails, rake her hair out and gain back what was mine but she acted so fond of me. Was it an act?

Damn, I was so paranoid, lost in my mind. I hadn't even noticed she had opened the kitchen door wide and I was exposed to them both. She was now two centimeters from me, smiling up at me like a housewife from the 50s. Her hand came up to my face, making me flinch back.

Her pretty pink lips popped open. "I'm sorry, you have a stray strand." She reached forward again and this time I let her and smiled my thanks, although I didn't mean it.

The doorbell rang again and Cade whipped her ass with a tea towel, making her squeal and rush for the door. His gaze lingered on mine as I watched her disappear.

"What are you thinking?" he asked, coming into my space. The hint of strawberries from his breath enticed me to move closer. I looked over his shoulder and saw he was slicing strawberries.

"I get it," I said boldly.

His lips lifted into a smile. He was gorgeous. How did I ever win his attention? "Get what, baby?"

"Amy."

He shook his head in confusion then nodded when he understood me. "Oh right, yeah. She tries to be respectful of your boundaries but there is something there and it's hard to fight." I felt my face drop, and with it what was left of my damaged heart. Ice washed through me, freezing over my soul. His huge palms gripped my face. "Faye, she would never do anything. You look ill."

"I . . . can't . . ."

He chuckled but it was a nervous one. "Babe, she has a girlfriend and she's not all of a sudden going to jump you. She's always had a thing for you. Damn, most of the world has. I didn't think it would make you that uncomfortable." *Wait. What?*

"Hey, you two, sorry to interrupt. This is Michelle, my girlfriend."

Holy shit! Knock me down with a feather.

I reached out to shake the blonde woman's hand as she bit her lip and jittered in front of me. "I'm a huge fan." She giggled, "Amy refused to bring me over so many times because she was worried I would fan girl on you."

My mouth was wide open, my eyes as wide and round, but no matter how much I tried to pull back my surprise, I couldn't.

"Are you okay?" she asked, concerned as she looked over the imperfections on my face; the bruises and cuts from Frank.

I snapped my mouth closed. "Oh, I. . . ."

"She just came from set, it's make-up. Now stop being nosey and let's go," Amy said. I gave her a small thank you smile. "I'm sorry, we have a dinner date and then I rushed over and . . ."

"It's fine, Amy. Michelle is welcome here with you anytime," Cade told her.

We waved them goodnight. Cade burst into a full out belly laugh.

"You son of a bitch!" I slapped his shoulder. "All this time you let me think she had a thing for you!" I screeched.

"I like you being jealous, it's a turn on," He smirked but then tensed and frowned. "I'm sorry I shouldn't."

He was afraid sex would be a topic that made me freeze and withdraw but he was so wrong. I didn't feel like a rape victim. In that moment, I felt like a survivor. We had been through so much, done so much. We were accessories to murder now. News spread about Dante's suspected death in the fire and the media had been stalking both mine and Cade's houses. I didn't want the life he stole me from anymore. I wanted a new one.

"I want to paint," I announced, taking Cade by surprise.

"Okay." He nodded encouragingly. "I have some of your equipment in one of the spare rooms."

I giggled and shook my head. "I mean, as my job. My full time job."

Placing his hands on my shoulders he looked deep in my eyes, searching them before his lips lifted into a breathtaking smile. "I want that too."

He meant our dream. The one we planned to have before all this. We would buy somewhere remote and far from the spotlight.

I returned his smile, its intensity making my jaw ache when it turned into a huge grin and I struggled to hold back the happy tears threatening to spill. Enough tears had been cried for many lifetimes and now was the time for food. "Feed me!"

He chuckled and pulled me into the kitchen.

EPILOGUE

NEW BEGINNINGS

Faye

IT HAD BEEN EIGHT WEEKS since escaping Dante. My poor agent who I had promoted before I went back to him was looking at me like I had grown two heads. "You want me to cancel all contracts?"

"I'm having a change in direction."

Theo was never found and after witnessing Dante murder Delia it was clear how capable of murder he was, and it gave me some comfort to know Theo was at the bottom of the ocean with Delia. They were sick people. A search was never launched for him. Documents from his recovered home computer had various offshore accounts on them, and plane tickets to Mexico. Kenny was leaving breadcrumbs just in case anyone did look into him dropping off the map.

I wrote my agent her final paycheck and added a juicy bonus that made her eyes and mouth pop open. She hugged me for a beat longer than acceptable and that was it, the last thing I needed to do.

My house was sold and everything I wanted to bring was packed. I didn't want to take any furniture, just some sentimental knick-knacks I had collected over the years. Everything there felt tainted by Frank and Dante.

I pushed through the large glass door for the last time and breathed in the fresh air, placing my oversized glasses on and walking to my car.

Cade would be home today. He'd had to go and help Jenson with something and was gone for a couple of nights. He made Kenny come and stay with me and as much as I loved him for everything he did for me, the image I walked in on when I first went to him for help played on repeat whenever I looked at him, and I blushed every time.

It took a few weeks for my wounds to heal, and the faint scarring on the top of my thighs from my own nails would forever be a reminder of what I went through, but Cade still looked at me like I was the most precious jewel he ever laid eyes on. He was reluctant to push me past kissing, and on occasion heavy petting, and I was going out of mind burning up for him. I knew everything that happened was just as hard on him and he also needed time, but sleeping next to a man carved to perfection was a kind of torture that was worse than any I had endured. His hair had grown a couple more inches and was long around his perfect face. I loved running my hands through it while he lay in my lap just watching a movie.

Beeeeep! Shit! I put my foot down on the green light and giggled to myself for zoning out at the traffic lights on thoughts of Cade.

I arrived back to his house and let myself in, dropping my bag on the stacked up pile of boxes by the front door. Kenny wasn't around, thank God. I told Sed, my bodyguard, who came in behind me to take the rest of the day off and made my way upstairs to shower. Cade still had me shadowed by a bodyguard which was necessary with my fans and the media.

I washed the day off my skin and stepped out of the shower, groaning when I saw no towel. We had packed most of the house up, only leaving the essentials, which according to Cade, was one towel to share. I had thrown the towel on the bedroom chair after last night's shower.

I pulled open the door and jumped a mile. A naked Cade stood there. I soaked him in, his tattoos coloring his strong muscular physique, his breathing causing his abs to ripple like a wave on the ocean. His hard cock was standing to greet me, a canvas with my name stamped there.

He didn't speak, he just walked over to me and pulled me by the wrist. Pushing my wet body down on to the mattress, his weight came down on top of me, his hard muscles pressing against my skin.

He ground his hard erection in to my pussy lips, causing a moan to rip free from my chest when it rubbed against my clit.

"You're so beautiful, Faye." His hands grasped the back of my neck before slipping up into my hair. His lips tasted mine in a frenzy of unrestrained lust. He broke the kiss to look me in the eye. "Put me inside you, baby."

I bit my lip to stop the intense passion and love I felt exploding in a torrent of tears and I love yous. I dragged my nails down his back before slipping round the front of him and gripping his hard length in my small hands, I stroked him a few times, worshipping the feel of him again in my hand.

His forehead came down to rest against mine so we could look down and watch our bodies join. I guided him to my opening and then wrapped my legs around his waist and dug my heels into his ass, pushing him inside me.

He slid in to me, both of us releasing a moan of satisfaction. His girth stretched and filled me in the most intoxicating way. Every part of me could feel him. His flesh molded to mine as we moved together, our eyes never leaving each other's.

I felt the muscles of his ass flex under my heel as I pushed him in deeper. His lips flanked mine as his elbows rested either side of my head to keep him from crushing me with his weight. I couldn't stop touching him. I never wanted to stop touching every naked inch of him.

He shifted upwards, cupping my waist. Rising to his knees, he brought me down on his hard cock so I was sitting on his lap. His arm wrapped tightly around my waist as the other cupped my chin in a firm hold. He held me hostage, adoring my mouth with his tongue and teeth. Our sweat guided our writhing movements. I lifted my hips and snapped them back down hard, grinding forward, then up and back down. My nipples rubbed against his chest with every thrust, his hips jerking forwards to meet me. It was getting harder and harder to breathe with my erratic panting. Warmth filled me, the fire in his eyes igniting me in an inferno of lust and need. I couldn't get close enough; I couldn't get him deep enough. He fed my appetite by dropping the hold on my face and moving between my thighs to pinch and caress my clit. My inner walls squeezed him, my body tensing and releasing the built up orgasm with cries of pleasure bursting from my lips as he followed me over, crying out my name as his hand dug into my skin just enough to leave a light mark.

He lowered us back down, his tongue lapping over the light spray of sweat glossing my skin. "I always remembered how your body tastes after sex but the memory doesn't do you justice." He shivered against my skin. His lips danced kisses down my torso before he dropped between my thighs, lifting my ass up so he could bury his face in my pussy. I was still sensitive so just his breath breathing sent me swirling. His tongue pushed inside me and then up to my clit. He lapped at me, devouring the release we just had together.

"And now that you're mine, so completely, our joining tastes even better."

I looked down at him, his eyes full of so much adoration as he looked up at me. My emotions swirled and I sucked in my lips as I tried to stop it from consuming me but when the sight of his own tears dripped down his face, I couldn't stop the torrent releasing. He leaned over the bed and slipped something from his jeans pocket. Bringing my hand up, he looped a piece of thread over my ring finger.

Cade shook his head, his own crying now matching mine. "I know we'll both forever miss the Dante we knew as kids. He was your first love, and he was my brother. But you know," he whispered as he climbed onto the bed and huddled me into him, keeping hold of the thread in one hand, "when we were kids, we made a promise to each other."

I turned into him, snuggling into his chest as I kept my eyes trained on his. "What was it?"

He smiled, more to himself than to me. "That we would die for each other."

I wrapped my free arm around him, holding onto his grief as he finally allowed it liberation, freeing him from the guilt. "And we both knew it was either him or me." He squeezed his eyes closed. "He gave up his for me. I know he did in the end. He knew, Faye, he knew he couldn't go on, that his life had ruined mine and yours."

"He did love you, Cade." I whispered, wiping his tears with my thumbs.

"Oh, I know." He nodded, mirroring my actions as he wiped at my tears. "It's funny. We took our first breaths together. And he took his last with me. But you, you are now the other beat to my heart, baby, the cadence that thumps in my chest."

I smiled, not having the words to express how much in love I was with this man.

"My heart now beats as two. Mine and Dante's before all this, and I will love you for both of us. So damn hard that you will forever feel the strength and love you deserved from him and me."

"After everything, you still honor him," I whispered in awe.

He smiled down at me. "Of course. He was the first one to ever take my hand, the first one I ever saw when I opened my eyes. His heart beat was the first thing I heard and his fingers were the first ones to ever touch me. He'll always live inside me, baby. Always."

I nodded. "He will always be with you, Cade. As he will always be with me, in our memories. But now it's our turn to take what he finally gave us."

He chuckled, tapping my nose. "I'm not sad, Faye. Don't think that's what I'm feeling. After everything he did, I still love him. He was a part of me. But I don't want to look back and remember the bad parts. That's what I'm saying. I want to remember him for what he gave me in the end."

"He gave me you too," I whispered, understanding him as he smiled down at me.

He nodded. "And if he hadn't taken you into his heart, then you wouldn't be laid here right now in mine. Things happen for a reason, Faye. I believe in fate. And fate took us on a journey that can never be changed, no matter how hard we try. So I just say, look back and smile because in the end we got here. And if it wasn't for Dante, then I wouldn't have the heart of the most beautiful woman on the planet. I wouldn't have her beautiful eyes staring up at me with so much love that I can feel it in my soul. I wouldn't have my ring on her finger."

I grinned up at him and bit my lip as I stared at the piece of thread. He chuckled and opened his palm for my ring to slide down.

"How did I ever deserve you?"

He shrugged, blinking back his tears as he took a deep breath. "You took the same journey, baby. We both deserve to be happy and you make me so damn happy." He leaned down, brushing his lips over mine. "Although, you can always show me just how grateful you are."

I chuckled, swinging my leg over him and rolling him over until I was straddled over his chest. "Oh, I'm very grateful. *Very grateful,*" I whispered as I traced over the tattoo on his left pectoral muscle with my finger, my name and his linked in a never ending circle. "But I'd do it all again, Cade, because memories are beautiful, even the bad ones." I reached down and stroked my finger over his lips. "Memories were once taken from me, my entire life a void. And now I even value the bad ones. But it's time to make new ones, ones that fill every single part of us that has been broken by this journey. It's time we filled each other with us."

He lifted a brow and I rolled my eyes, shaking my head and chuckling at his humor.

"And I'm all for filling you up, baby." He smirked.

And with that, he rolled me back over and filled me with even more memories, memories that I would cherish forever. Memories that we deserved.

THE END

KEEP READING FOR A SNEAK PEEK
AT THE UPCOMING NOVELLA

A Deception Novella

Jenson

HE WAS A SLIMY FUCKER. He was like Bin Laden, going in to hiding when the shit hit the fan and the war came to him! The thing about depraved underworld-dealing filth, there were no friends amongst criminals.

It took eight weeks but finally we found someone willing to talk for the right amount of money and that was something I wasn't lacking in. Beneath Innocence were at the height of our fame, a world tour planned for the next six months, but first I needed this last act, this last piece of unfinished business.

Liam had taken Blue home with him after a four week stay in hospital, much to my shock. She had lived here with her mom her whole life, but her mom died a few years back and she was pretty much alone. She didn't even look at me when she left and took with her my still beating heart. Which was a good thing. I needed to have no heart for this.

I promised Liam I would get the job finished and he helped me track down the right people to squeal Hunter's whereabouts. I thanked Cade for helping me with this one last thing before he went to start his new life with Faye and closed the door.

I turned to look into the eyes of a man who sent out punishers to do unspeakable acts without any remorse and I wouldn't show him any in his death.

I brushed my hands over the tools set out on the table he was strapped to. The thing about witnessing torture and being part of it, you either get a taste for it or you become a victim of it in your head. I wouldn't let anything own me so I owned it! And let the pleasure in revenge feed me.

I picked up a small but deadly scalpel. "This one's for Slicer." I smiled. . . .

Beneath Innocence
Coming Soon
From Ker Dukey & D H Sidebottom

Printed in Great Britain
by Amazon.co.uk, Ltd.,
Marston Gate.